PREFACE

A brief history of the Dragon Flights and the Wars in the years before the book begins (optional reading)

Once over, the five dragon flights created courts in their lands and built the city of Reodian as the center of the dragon realm. The Emerald, Ruby, Sapphire, Ivory, and Ebon First-Born ruled over their respective courts aided by their exarch princes, and the flights lived harmoniously with each other.

The dragons kept themselves isolated from the neighboring human and elven lands. Although the other two races distrusted the dragons' secretive society, the three co-existed in the world they shared.

Over a hundred years ago, infighting between the dragons led to the Wars. The Queen of the Ebon battled the other flights in her quest for dominion over all courts. Nobody knows what provoked the Ebon First-Born to turn against the other elders after years of peace, but the war spilled over into the rest of the lands.

Old prejudices between the dragons and their neighbors re-emerged, and so did the dragon's claim that they once owned all the lands. Thus, the flights not only fought each other but also battled with the humans and elves. During the Wars, the dragons moved Reodian to a place of safety, and so the city survived the destruction. Now the city can only be reached by magic and humans and elves rarely enter.

Ultimately, all the flights were destroyed, including the Ebon.

The Ebon Queen, Lyrandra, was determined to reclaim the human and elven lands. Even before her flight fell, she recruited and then corrupted elves to aid in her war. These so-called Ebon elves pledged their loyalty in return for the magic she gifted them. They created their own court and assisted her in fighting against the peaceful Lumen elves and humans. These elves also lost their Lumen elven looks and grew to match the Ebon flight's coloring. Lyrandra then created powerful Daughters of Shadow to aid her and taught them shadowmancy.

None outside her court saw the Ebon Queen in person, and all believed her to be an elven sorceress who had taken the title after the dragon elder died. Lyrandra's enemies were unaware the First-Born Ebon dragon survived and that she had a male consort who aided her.

The corrupt Ebon magic brought decay that began to eat through the lands. The Lumen elven courts were ruined, forcing many to take sanctuary with the humans. The human lands were gradually engulfed too. These new allies, led by the human kingdom's Silvercrest troops, fought the Ebon for many years. They found and killed the Daughters of Shadow, but the Queen's magic was too great against their armies.

Rumors spread that dragons still existed and slumbered, but none outside their society knew what secrets the dragons kept. Before the Ebon Queen destroyed the flights, the four other elders' essences were stored and hidden. Only their return would be enough to kill the Ebon Queen, but they could only be rebirthed by one with a dragon soul. As most believed no dragons existed, this became a folk tale.

Twenty-one years ago, a dragon emerged from hiding and led a party of humans and elves to the eggs containing the elders, including a human woman with a dragon soul. She rebirthed the four flights' First-Born, and with her help, the elders destroyed the Ebon Queen and her consort. Most believe that the Ebon First-Born's essence was lost in the battle.

The death of the Ebon Queen ended the Wars. Now, the humans and elves have a shaky alliance with the dragons and all are rebuilding their lands. The First-Born have recreated their exarchs and reinstated the courts. Those Ebon who survived the corruption are accepted back into elven society. All races' leaders agree that the Ebon flight can never be allowed to return. They cannot risk such death and destruction again.

The First-Born dragons are the only leaders who know the truth—the human woman, Calla, now contains some of the Ebon elder's essence. Because Calla has a bond to a dragon and that is sacred to the flights, the other elders permitted her to live. She now resides within an elven court under their watch. The dragons continue to oversee Calla for signs of corrupt magic.

Recently, the First-Born suspect that there may be somebody else in the realms who possesses more than Ebon essence—they believe the Ebon First-Born's soul exists.

The human woman had a daughter, and the family hid her from the dragon elders.

The dragons want to find her.

CHARACTERS IN THE DRAGON'S REBORN SERIES

MAIN CHARACTERS

Aurelia: *human daughter of the Aureate Court*
Velanor: *Ruby flight exarch*
Camanor: *Sapphire flight exarch*
Elianor: *Ivory flight exarch*
Lucanor: *Emerald flight exarch*

AURELIA'S FAMILY

Calla: *the human Lady of the Aureate Court*
Galen: *High Elf of the Aureate Court (Lumen elf)*
Leander: *High Lord and human leader of the Silvercrest stronghold armies*
Rohan: *human knight of the Silvercrest stronghold*
Devin: *an elven mercenary and 'Swiftblade' (Ebon elf)*
Luin: *dragon of the Sapphire Flight and 'The Guardian'*

DRAGON FIRST-BORN ELDERS

Talindra: *the Ruby Queen*
Delanor: *the Sapphire King*
Aelinor: *the Ivory King*
Kalinor: *the Emerald King*
Lyrandra: *the Ebon Queen (deceased)*

NOTABLE PLACES

Aureate Court: *Calla and Galen's home, and Aurelia's childhood home*
Reodian: *the central dragon city*
Silvercrest Stronghold: *Leander's and Rohan's home*
Westport: *Aurelia and Devin's port town home*
The Scorched Lands: *the still-damaged part of the Ruby court*
The North Wastes: *suspected Ebon territory at the edges of the Ivory court*

CHAPTER I

AURELIA

THE DRAGONS RARELY VISIT WESTPORT AND TONIGHT THE sapphire-haired stranger will wish he hadn't. His welcome won't be warm. Humans trust the race even less than the elves since every time a dragon appears in town, they seduce their way into the beds of the wealthy, separate them from their coin and jewels—then leave.

This one took no time to disguise what he is, his blue hair touching his ears rather than hidden beneath the hood of his cloak. Not that dragons can hide who they are; no man reaches their height and bulk, which is the reason no man challenges them when they appear in my hometown.

The dragon lounges in the corner, aware none would dare approach, long, black-clad legs stretched in front, empty wine bottle on his table, keen eyes watching every arrival.

Waiting for somebody?

This port town filled with thieves and degenerates would be a world away from the dragon city Reodian. This rough establishment falls short of the opulence he's accustomed to within the dragon flights' rebuilt realm. The inn's patrons aren't the humans that dragons usually target; he'll find little of worth if he takes one of these people home.

I sit alone in a darkened corner favored by those in my line of work, and I'm safe from the dragon's touch. Not only because my blade is as keen as the dragon's eyes but because my father would slit a throat as soon as any man looked at me the wrong way. Nobody ever confirmed that Devin is the notable assassin Swiftblade, but none take the risk.

They know not to tangle with his daughter for this reason alone, and now I'm an adult and have my father's skills, people are more likely to employ me than assault me. The blade nestles against my hip tonight, beneath the long cloak and against the dark leather pants I always wear. No pretty dresses for me; I won't constrain myself or my body.

A nobleman who claims a Sapphire dragon violated his daughter and ransacked his home offered me a tempting amount of coin to use my expertise on him. I know the girl in question, and she was not violated—Rosanna was a willing participant who underestimated the primal creature's forceful fucking.

Rosanna's usual lovers treat her with romance and gentleness as they attempt to worm their way into the noble family; the dragons only care about fucking and thieving. She also confided in me that she enjoyed the night but couldn't tell anybody she'd lain with a dragon. When the rumors reached her father's ears, she maintained her innocence and swore that he seduced her.

And so, I've scouted for a Sapphire dragon and found this one, easily identifiable as belonging to that flight. Sapphire, Ruby, Emerald, or Ivory—members of the different dragon flights are unmistakable since each has hair color to match that of their dragon form.

Once, dark-haired Ebon dragons lived too but their Ebon Queen started a war that destroyed dragons, elves, and human lives and land. Now she's dead and the Ebon flight no longer exists.

My mother killed her.

I've taken time to study this dragon—the arrogant smile constantly playing around his full mouth, the sharp features and square jaw, and the unusual, deep cerulean eyes that intensify this man's unnatural state. Muscles strain against the tight pants he wears, his thigh twice the width of my slender leg, and he taps sharp nails on the table.

Seduced.

I understand the attraction that some have towards shifted dragons—those who can see beyond our violent history with the race, and their superior nature. Especially if they enjoy a man with primal power humming around him or the thrill from lying with illicit lovers.

The dragons' weakness for sex will help tonight because this one appears to have chosen an appetizer before his main course; a morsel before he moves to a wealthier establishment and woman.

Clara, the youngest barmaid in the tavern at twenty years old has fallen under his spell. A literal spell? Dragons possess magic, offensive as far as I know, and perhaps they've more than body and charm to achieve their aims. Aware he'd seek out the youngest, prettiest woman, I offered Clara coin to aid my plan. We'll swap identities. I'm female and can pretty myself should I need, and I'm as slender as she is although a touch taller, so exchanging places with her should be easy.

The dragon will barely get his shifted paws on me before I introduce him to my blade. Tonight, I chose the dagger I named Dragonsbane because when drunk one night, Devin told me the weapon's history. He killed an Ebon flight dragon with the weapon—the *last* male dragon of the Ebon flight and the Queen's consort. Perhaps the short-bladed weapon is infused with luck and charm from previous use and will aid me in killing this one.

The dragon takes a ridiculous amount of time stalking his prey, and I grow frustrated. I could've spent the evening on a speedier, although less lucrative, task but remind myself the reward will be worth every bored moment waiting.

Rebecca walks over, the tavern owner's wife who hides her years behind a painted face, graying hair swept into a now-loosening bun. "Not working tonight?" she asks and places down two glasses before pouring generous servings of rum and taking one.

"Later." This larger woman blocks my view of the dragon and I fidget, wanting to look past her but not for my move to appear obvious.

"I hope your mark isn't the gentleman with *sapphire* hair." Rebecca drinks the whole glass in one go and pushes the other towards me. I suck my lips together and look away. "Ria. Don't be stupid."

Looking back, I sip the rum. "Who says I'm here to kill the creature? Maybe I'm curious and want to fuck a dragon?"

She splutters. "As rebellion against Devin?"

I run my tongue across my top teeth as her comment stings. Twenty-one years old and he still attempts to father me like I'm young. "I'm a big girl now, Becca. I don't need to rebel like a child."

With a sigh, Rebecca perches on the edge of the sticky table and leans in to pour another measure of rum. "Clara already has him in her sights. The size of her!" She clicks her tongue. "He'll eat her alive."

"Perhaps that's what she wants?" I suggest.

"The race are a lot of things, but they don't eat humans." I smirk and she shakes her head. "Whatever he wants from her, that man isn't a common dragon, Ria. She needs to be careful."

"I'm aware he's dragon nobility; they have the strongest traits when pretending they're civilized men." I bare my teeth to indicate another thing I noticed—his teeth are sharper.

"They don't pretend to be anything and are not men." She stands again. "Dragons have two forms. That's all."

Clara's cloaked figure catches my eye as she squeezes past two burly men blocking her way through to behind the bar. My teeth grate as one of them grabs her ass. If they try that when *I'm* Clara… I shake my head. Nothing, because I can't draw attention to myself.

"Excuse me." I hastily stand and maneuver my way through the crammed tavern.

One of the handsy men appraises me as I approach, and I tip my chin so he can see who's beneath the hood. He scowls in recognition and drinks his ale.

Clara peers at me and I pull her into the small storeroom adjoining the kitchen, that's crammed with crates and empty barrels, cooking ingredients in bottles on alcove shelves. She wears her hair in a braid down her back and I set about braiding mine. Due to my unfortunate looks inherited from my father, my blue-black hair doesn't match Clara's, but in the dark this will be hard to distinguish from her deeper brown. As will my eyes, again an uncommon violet-blue, slightly different to the green Ebon.

I've faced prejudice my whole life for looking like the dark elves who turned against their Lumen brethren. Calling themselves Ebon despite having no Ebon flight powers, they fought for the Queen, and were gifted magic in return for their loyalty.

The Ebon elves who escaped corruption rejoined our society after the Wars, and they're accepted but not trusted.

The Ebon flight and all their evil may be gone, but the taint of the name hasn't.

My father isn't Ebon either, his looks an unfortunate throwback to his ancestors, but he faces the same prejudice.

"I'll need your dress," I say as I finish braiding and pull my loose grey tunic over my head.

Her mouth drops open as she averts her eyes from my undergarments. "You never told me such!"

"We're the same size. What's the problem?" I beckon at her to do as I ask. "If the dragon is pursuing you, he'll know how you're dressed. And if he's noticed me, he'll know how *I'm* dressed." Clara's eyes widen further when I produce my concealed dagger and place the blade on the floor as I kick off my boots and drag down my pants. "I'm paying you for this, remember?"

Clara unhooks her heavy, navy cloak and pushes it onto a shelf before turning away and shyly unlacing her green and white dress. Why shyly? I'm definitely not the first to see Clara half-naked. Her back remains to mine as the simple cotton dress slips to her ankles and she steps out. I push my clothes towards her by the toe before taking the long dress and pulling on the garment. Stale beer and rosewater smelling. Ugh.

When did I last wear a dress? Last time I pretended to be a lady, which isn't often. Normally only when forced to attend a party arranged by my human mother and my other father, a Lumen elf. Galen enjoys holding parties and does so often as the High Elf of the Aureate Court. Hence my name, as if Aurelia would wipe away the dark Ebon looks and turn me into a golden child.

Other father. I have four but live with Devin for a life away from the court's attention and their fussing. This isn't unusual for elves but shocking to humans that my mother has many men.

"What did you speak to the dragon about?" I ask as I shove my breasts into the bodice and scowl at how much the dress displays as I tighten the laces.

"Not much. He only asked my name and if I wanted to accompany him to his lodgings." She chuckles. "They're always forthright."

"Have you accompanied a dragon to lodgings before?" Clara turns, now half-dressed in my tunic and pants, and I arch a brow.

"No!" She pulls a disgusted face as I snatch her cloak from the shelf and swing it around my shoulders. "He told me his name. Camanor."

Cama*nor*. This means he's definitely the correct mark as the 'nor' confirms that he's a purer bred dragon—or pretending to be one. "Useful. Thank you."

Clara looks at me awkwardly and bites her lip. I smile and pat my hip before pointing to hers. "Payment? The coin is in your pocket. Take the pouch but I'll return for my clothes later. Do you have the rosewater?" My eyes go to the line of brown bottles. "Behind there?" She nods.

I reach behind a jar of pickled onions and pull out a smaller clear bottle with light pink liquid inside then unscrew the cap.

"Why do you need that?" she asks as I splash some of the overpowering perfume across my exposed skin.

"Dragons have a keen sense of smell. I won't smell the same as you." I pass her the bottle. "I do now."

Fastening the cloak, I then yank the hood until my face is shrouded. My dagger lies at my feet, and I slip on her boots before sliding Dragonsbane inside one, the ebony carving familiar in my hand. I'd know this dagger even in the dark.

"Good luck," she mumbles.

I snort. Mr. Sapphire needs the good luck.

CHAPTER 2

AURELIA

CAMANOR STANDS THE MOMENT I WALK THROUGH THE INN with my head bowed, and I peer at him from beneath the hood as I navigate my way through the tables, boots sticking to the ale-soaked floor.

He slants his head, eyes gleaming despite the dim light. "Why hide your pretty face? Are you frightened somebody will see you with a dragon?"

He has a sonorous edge to his low tone, the words spoken differently to a human—slower, more deliberate. The only dragon, I've stood this close to before is Luin who lives with my mother and Galen at their court. Ironically, Luin is Sapphire flight too but doesn't visit their realm often.

Dragons hold a physical presence that's inevitable for a creature this size, but I never expected to be instantly mesmerized, as I look back into his eyes. "No, I'm not worried," I whisper. "But leave quickly."

A whisper may disguise my voice, but there's too much

light in this dingy room and if Camanor looks any closer he may see I've different features than Clara—a face shaped closer to an elf's, with eyes a touch larger than human.

Without waiting for a response, I duck past a group of loud men who've supped too much tonight and rush through the door. I hesitate outside and Camanor is forced to stoop to follow me through the doorway into the muggy night.

From the inn's vantage point high up in the town, the docks are visible. Tonight, Westport holds ships of varying sizes, from small boats for local fishermen to galleons with large crews who travel to the furthest lands for the most expensive goods to trade. The shadowed outlines create a silhouetted tableau against the seas, lights shining from within some vessels adding a prettiness to a usually not-pretty place.

The cobbled pathway at the edge of the street descends towards the docks or ascends towards the outskirts of town. Westport is an unsavory place in all aspects, including many residents, and not a place many walk at night. A short stroll down a winding route and we reach a narrower pathway with brick and wood buildings squashed together, the houses' eaves almost touching those opposite. I'm accustomed to the stench from so many living in proximity, but Camanor covers his mouth and nose.

Oh, the things he must suffer in order to thieve from or fuck humans. Poor thing.

"You barely speak to me," the dragon says. "Do I worry you?" I shake my head. "Hmm. Follow."

Camanor strides away and I hurry to do as he says. His boots are heavy, footsteps loud on the stones but my soft-soled footwear quiet. We follow the street downwards into a dingier part of town until he pauses by a door. I look up. This isn't a public resting place but a home, clothing hanging from the window above to dry. I no longer dry my clothes outside —every item smells of fish when I do.

This isn't somewhere I'd expect a dragon to stay—there are better establishments with more comforts and more choice of women.

"I like the full Westport experience," he says as if reading my thoughts, and I tense as sharper teeth glint when he smiles. "Aren't you concerned I'll harm you?" When I don't answer, he opens the unlocked door and again needs to bend to fit his muscular frame through. Camanor turns his head to watch as I step inside. "No. Evidently you're not concerned," he says with amusement.

I adjust my eyes to the dim. A single oil lantern burns on the wall, and I can make out the shape of narrow stairs leading upwards. A typical Westport home with one downstairs room and no doubt only one above, although the stove in this room would be lit and the table covered with plates. Who does this dwelling belong to?

Camanor reaches behind me to pull the front door closed, leaning over me to do so, and his scent washes over me, a fresh, earthy smell as if he stepped from a mist-covered woods. As his arm brushes mine, I'm surprised by the heat of his skin compared to my goose-bumped flesh in the cool dwelling.

But the goosebumps are more than the cold. He places hands behind his back and bends slightly. "Is your decision to join me curiosity, Clara? Or have you heard how dragons fuck and want to confirm how pleasurable we are?"

I swallow. How long until I can distract him and reach into my boot? I've taken on large assailants before—both large human men and the Garn from the distant lands. They're human but much broader than any in our lands, and always visit our realm with ill intent.

As a child, Devin had me practice combat with Rohan,

the notable Silvercrest guard who who visits my mother at the Aureate court—another father. My family were always intent on teaching me to fight from as young as I can remember.

I step back as Camanor reaches for my hood and he chuckles before reaching to place long fingers against my neck. "You will need to uncover more than your face for me."

"Then I prefer to be with you in the dark," I whisper.

"You're shy?" He snorts. "I can see enough to be sure that there's nothing distasteful about your body."

Ugh.

"Do you have a bed?" Is my whispering strange to him or does he believe I'm nervous?

"A bed? And what if dragons don't fuck in beds, Clara?" His fingers move towards the skin at the top of my breasts; I shiver against the soft touch and the deep warmth when they linger a moment. "Perhaps I'll hold you against that door and satisfy your curiosity right here and now."

In answer, I shuffle away from the door, and he barks out a laugh. "Very well. We'll use the bed."

The uneven stairs are difficult for me to navigate in the dark, but Camanor has no problems as he stomps upwards. I glance around. Two other doors, one either side of the small landing. Shit. I didn't factor in one thing—are others here?

"We're alone," he says, by way of answer to my silent question.

The room we walk into is larger than mine at the dwelling I share with Devin but still seems cramped, especially with a dragon sharing the space. I'm barely in the room before Camanor pulls down my hood and jerks my face to his. I prepare myself for the moment he spots I'm not Clara but instead his mouth claims mine.

I'm caught by surprise and steady myself with one hand on his chest. He shoves the door closed and the dragon presses me against the wood, one hand tangled in my hair, his hips holding me in place. My lips part, body reacting even though my mind shouts at me to push him away—until I lose my mind completely, the dragon's touch and taste wiping my thoughts.

Camanor's tongue pushes roughly against mine and I grasp his neck, reacting to his insistent lust with the same force. This dragon engulfs me with a kiss deeper and harder than any I've had before, and I'm overwhelmed in a way I never thought possible as I yield to his hands and mouth, a primal part of me wanting him. We lock together as if something within us both now aches to meet.

He grips my waist and turns around, falling onto me as I hit the bed. I gasp into his mouth but don't stop, hands moving beneath his tunic and meeting stone-like muscle. I'm insane but my blood sings with desire as both of his hands slide beneath my skirts, harsh fingers running along my leg from ankle to thigh. Shit, he's about to discover how aroused I am—and what's worse, I'm happy for him to.

Am I really that starved for attention?

One of the dragon's hands moves away while his sharper nails on the other bite into my ass, holding me against him, his hard cock pushing between us. The weight and heat of him engulfs me as his other hand slides up my body until a large palm covers my breasts. As abruptly as it started, Camanor's kiss ends and he dips his head, pulling at the laces of my dress, tracing his tongue downwards.

He breathes heavily, almost growling as he parts my legs with his knee, getting closer and closer to my heavy breasts. Closing my eyes, I hold his head, not sure where I am any longer as he yanks at the front of my dress and flicks my nipple with his tongue.

The fingers on my ass slide across my belly and he dips

one lower, skimming my undergarments. Air hisses through his teeth.

What in the stars name do dragons use to cause humans to behave like this? Once, someone gave me rum laced with herbs that altered my mind and caused this reaction, but I've only drunk what Rebecca offered. This physical reaction to Camanor goes far beyond one simply caused by herbs.

In a swift move, Camanor snatches both my wrists in one hand and pins my arms above my head. I wrench my mouth from his, pulling against the biting grip. "What are you doing?"

The dragon's bright silver eyes glow in the dim, his weight remaining on me. "What's the matter, Aurelia? I thought you wanted me to *satisfy* your curiosity."

Oh. Fuck. "Who?"

"Forget the pretense, you wicked girl. I'm perfectly aware who you are." He holds my wrists in one hand and reaches for something beside him. "And because I know who you are..." The point of a dagger almost touches my face. *My* dagger. "I won't use this on the easily seduced so-called assassin."

"I am not easily seduced." I writhe against him, but his hold tightens.

Camanor's mouth almost touches mine again as he speaks. "Is that so? Then why are you half-naked in bed with the dragon you planned to kill several minutes ago? Aroused, imagining how good a dragon's cock would feel if you fucked him?"

He dips his head and captures my lip between his sharp teeth. Along with his weight, the cock he mentioned presses against me, confirming one rumor about the size of dragons.

Control yourself, Ria. This creature has more weapons than a dagger.

A breath rushes out as he stands. "A pleasure which I will not give you."

13

Snatching my chance, I roll from the bed and pull the dress back over my breasts before lurching towards the door. Massive arms circle my waist and pull me backwards, caging me against his chest. The blade he still holds doesn't press against my throat, but I'm aware of his labored breathing and his arousal against my back.

"If we had time, perhaps I *would* satisfy you and myself." He nips my ear. "But I'm expecting someone else to join us."

I struggle again. "Another dragon? Let me go!"

Camanor's spare hand slides upwards and circles my throat, tipping my head backwards. The silver eyes shine brighter than ever, made more sinister by the dragon's slit pupil. "No."

He spins me around and I back towards the door as he places the dagger between his teeth and reaches towards my breasts again. I'm about to slap his hand away when he begins to lace up what he quickly unlaced minutes ago. His fingers and sharper nails drag across my skin sending a reminder of his rougher touch.

Camanor takes the dagger in a hand again before drawing me close. "I wouldn't like him to know what you almost did, Aurelia. Sit with me."

Him?

He walks backwards still holding tight and sits on the one chair in the room, beneath the thinly draped window, pulling me firmly onto his lap. Hot breath strokes my neck and I'm pissed that I'm imagining him parting my legs and continuing his touch.

The dragon doesn't speak, holding me firmly around the waist, not touching anywhere else. Only the sound of our slowing breathing fills the room along with the moonlight.

A door to the house slams and somebody runs up the stairs.

Another dragon?

I struggle against his banded arms again, but the person who appears in the doorway isn't a dragon. My heart drops into my boots as I gawk at the elf in leathers and a thick cloak, his rough cut hair more human in style than long, elven locks.

Devin.

His dark Ebon features are filled with a malevolent fury I rarely see from him, a look many must've received before his dagger ended them and I take a shuddery breath. I'm unsure who his anger is aimed at. Me or Camanor?

"Ah. Devin. Now we're both here, perhaps you could explain your deception," Camanor says evenly, and I'm mortified I'm still in his lap.

Why hasn't Devin drawn his blade? He never walks anywhere without one. "What deception?" I ask.

"Did you touch her?" Devin growls, appraising my looser braid and flushed face.

"Only a little. She's a temptress." Camanor rubs his nose along my neck. "I'd love to taste her dragon soul."

Finally, his grip loosens, and I manage to stand on wobbling legs.

With a smirk at me, Camanor runs a finger across his lips and his gaze dips below my waist. "Amongst other things."

Devin growls again.

I twist my head between them, mind reeling.

Camanor stands too and claps my father on the shoulder. "We shall leave Westport tonight; in case you're tempted to hide Aurelia again."

"What the fuck is happening?" I interrupt.

The dragon drops my dagger to the floor and brushes his hands together as if the thing was covered in muck. Scowling, Devin squats down to pick up the weapon.

"Devin. I hope you don't share Aurelia's earlier intention

to shiv me." Camanor's tone is lazy; he knows the answer to his question.

"I'm not accustomed to killing arbitrarily," Devin replies. He continues to stare at me in disappointment and I avert my eyes.

"And because I'd rip you apart before you so much as touched me." Camanor flashes his teeth. "Yes, I'm aware you once killed a dragon, but that was pure luck."

Devin's anger firmly switches to Camanor. "You know nothing of my history."

"I know enough that if you prevent me returning to the First-Born with Aurelia, you'd bring trouble for the Aureate court and perhaps a diplomatic incident nobody wants." He smirks. That damn *smirk*.

The First-Born dragon elders? They live in the dragon realm far from here and I'm not going to that place. Big no. "Dev. Can we leave?" I ask him and attempt to move from Camanor who pulls me back again.

"Did you expect your father to stride in and rescue you?" Camanor murmurs against my ear as if hearing my thoughts. "Do you know why he hasn't?"

"Don't," warns Devin.

"Because, Aurelia, your father isn't here. Devin is not him, and you're not half-elf." I look in bewilderment at Devin. "Take us to the Aureate court, elf, and we shall discuss this further."

"I'm sorry, but what the fuck are you saying? Who is my father?" I interrupt, attempting to keep my voice angry and not fearful. *Not half-elf.* That rules out Galen too. "If not you or Galen, who?" I ask them both.

Camanor shrugs. "That doesn't matter."

"It matters to me!" I half-shout, and the Sapphire asshole arches a brow. My mother's human men? "Is Leander or Rohan my father, Devin?" But... I tense. Camanor said dragon soul. "Not *Luin*. How could my mother possibly breed with a dragon?"

"We're all your father," Devin says quietly. "You know that."

Perhaps, but my family have lied to me for my whole life. Now a dragon has found me and torn through the secrecy.

Why?

CHAPTER 3

AURELIA

DEVIN NEITHER CONFIRMED NOR DENIED CAMANOR'S claim and ignored my repeated questions as we traveled the half day to the Aureate court. I grew angry, shouting that he owed me an explanation, but he adopted his shuttered elven attitude, merely informing me that until our whole family is together, he can't explain further. Pissed with him, I rode on ahead and refused to speak to him about anything.

Devin following a dragon's orders is enough to worry me what might happen if I don't, because very little bothers Devin and he bows to nobody.

Camanor arrives at the court much earlier than us—the benefit of flight—and I'd love to know what happened as he set foot in court and explained why. I resided here until twelve years of age because Devin traveled often with his 'work'. If he were in the realm, my family would pack me off to his home in Westport—the place a jarring contrast from the aesthetic beauty found within an elven court.

As I grew older, the questions grew too. Why did my mother not live with Devin, my father? Why did my visits to him coincide with visits from strangers to the court?

I've heard the stories; how people feared and still fear my mother Calla for the dark Ebon magic infused in her as a child. Yes, she used this to defeat the Ebon flight's queen, but the humans won't accept that she's harmless. They fear she'll use Ebon sorcery and Calla lives within Galen's court for protection. And so, I long believed that the reason High Lord Silvercrest frequently visited was on behalf of the humans—an exercise to check on Calla for signs of dark magic.

Until I saw my mother kissing him and his hands up her skirts.

Not what a ten-year-old should see but I shouldn't sneak around the house to avoid my tutor. This incident wasn't as shocking as the morning I came across the lightbringer knight, Rohan leaving her chamber and when I burst in to see her, now convinced she'd be alone, High Lord Silvercrest was in her bed.

I'd long thought that something odd happened between her and my father that kept him away, and I'd already grown suspicious that Galen may be her new lover, but never dreamed of this. That day, Calla sat me down and explained she had many lovers and how this isn't unusual within an elven court.

But my mother isn't an elf.

Well, I don't think so, but following the dragon's news about my father, I'm no longer sure.

My biggest shock that day? One of my mother's lovers is the dragon who spent the first years of my life following me everywhere and scolding me often. Luin never raised a hand to me but would never allow me to travel into the town alone. I longed for the days I could escape to Westport for time with Devin. Luin would stay at the court because dragons aren't welcome in Westport, and I'd enjoy freedom in Devin's un-courtly world.

One day, as a young child, I told Luin that I hated him and wished he would leave. The dragon rarely shows any emotion, but I instantly regretted speaking because the hurt from my barbed words filled his silver eyes.

Later, I told my mother what happened, and she explained the way of dragons—how Luin loves and protects what's most precious to him but struggles to apply human niceties. She also promised to talk to Luin, and his attitude softened.

A little.

Devin would joke that the men I now consort with should be happy that Luin knows nothing. Because if he did, his protectiveness would escalate into violence against any man who touched his daughter.

Now, as I stand in Galen's formal room, I attempt to read those silver eyes again. But he doesn't meet mine, instead staring at Camanor as impassively as ever.

Is *he* my real father?

Who is?

What have these people already spoken about?

Every member of my family is gathered in the sitting room, as if this were a casual meeting—no doubt Galen's attempt to de-escalate a situation. My mother Calla sits on a white upholstered sofa with Galen beside her in front of the silver-barked tree, a symbol of the Lumen elves' closely held link to the nature goddesses.

As a child, I found myself in trouble a few times for climbing the tree in the center of the room. This is the court's oldest and grows through the white marble floor, branches spreading throughout the house, the Aureate ancestors buried beneath the home and close to the roots.

That's what caused trouble—the court elves were

horrified at my disrespect. Galen was good-natured about the situation, citing how young I was and that I didn't understand. Instead, he moved my chambers to the top of the home where I could sit in the bowers.

So, I found different trees to climb outside only this time with Luin fussing that I might fall.

Galen, with his long-white hair always dresses in fine, colorful clothes and once I asked why he looked so silly compared to Rohan and Leander. Rohan stood close by at the time, in his dark pants and tunic covered in mud from our tussling and couldn't hide his laughter. I look to the tall, broad-chested man now, who stands in the window arms crossed. Rohan's thick brown hair dips into a face that's pinched with annoyance, as I expected from him.

Leander stands one side of the sofa, hands in his pockets. Has he only recently arrived? Because he's wearing his blue cloak, pinned with the Silvercrest emblem but isn't dressed as a High Lord, more like Rohan's simple clothes he travels in. I know him well, and if he's facing confrontation or political matters, Leander ensures people clearly see his position in our realms.

Luin stands stiffly the other side, one hand resting on the back of the seat, close to my mother's blonde head. We couldn't be more different; her fair skin and gentle human features the opposite to my blue-black hair and dark lilac eyes. I'm more human than elf in appearance, but I have traits that make me deceptively sweet-looking.

But Luin is the one I can't help staring at. I'm aware that my mother shares her bed with him too but surely they couldn't have a baby? I'd *surely* have blue hair like him and Camanor? As usual, Luin's unreadable but his eyes are now fixed on the other dragon. I'm surprised Luin hasn't pummeled him yet.

I take a seat opposite them, and Calla shakes her head at

me as I prop my dirty boots on Galen's shining marble table. With a huff, I place them on the floor.

I want these people to see exactly how angry and upset I am. I'm furious with all of them including Camanor for his role in flipping my life upside down. He sits across from me, tipping his mouth into a knowing smile and dipping his eyes to my lips.

I pull a sour face.

Luin watches.

But I swear Camanor knows how intensely I react to his presence, even meters away, and not touching. Is that what a dragon's kiss does to a girl? Brands her with something that makes him irresistible?

"Which one of you is my father?" I demand the moment we're gathered.

"All of them, Ria," says Calla softly. "We discussed this."

"Yes. But which one *fathered* me?" I look from one man to another. "Whose blood runs in my veins?"

"Oh, your blood isn't the issue," says Camanor. "Rather, your essence."

I blink. "Essence? You mean the person I am?"

"No." He shakes his head and looks to Calla as he waves a hand. "I understand why you hid Ria from the First-Born, but how could you expect that no dragon would discover her?"

My back straightens as if somebody jammed a steel rod down my spine. "Hid me from the First-Born?" The dragon elders—the originals who all other dragons descend from. One from each flight and four entities who personify the very nature of their race—arrogant, unyielding, and unforgiving. Especially the Ruby Queen.

No... "You're a First-Born?" I jab a finger at Camanor.

His annoying laugh rumbles from him. "You flatter me, but Talindra wouldn't allow any of her consorts to lie with another. And last night when we—"

"What?" interrupts Luin sharply and stands. "If you took Aurelia to your bed..." Calla pulls on his tunic sleeve.

"A gentleman never tells." Camanor smirks again.

"Gentleman? Ha. And no, I did not," I retort. "Don't you think I'd have bruises?"

Rohan's lips thin. "I hope you're speaking the truth, Ria."

"Truth? You've not answered my question." I cross my arms.

"We don't know, Aurelia. Only that Devin is certainly not." Galen moves to crouch in front of me, and his cool gold rings touch my skin as he takes my hand.

"Why 'certainly not'? Don't you fuck Devin, mother?" I retort.

"Aurelia!" Leander stares at me in shock then jerks his head around to Devin and snarls, "Such language and disrespect for her mother! Our daughter spends too much time around your lowlife accomplices."

"Sorry," I mumble and squeeze back tears. "I'll guard my tongue, but I can't help how upset I am by your lies."

Calla crosses to perch on the seat beside me and takes my other hand between both of hers, almost triggering the tears I'm holding back.

"Why did you lie to me?" I ask, voice thick.

Not only do I sense her sorrow but see evidence in her face; eyes reddened by earlier tears and her happy aura missing. "To keep you safe, Ria," she says and her eyes well again. "I'm sorry."

"Why would I look this way if Devin isn't my father? None other has Ebon elf features."

"Hmm. Interesting question." Camanor rests his elbow on the arm of the chair, fist beneath his chin. "I'm eager to hear your answer, my friends."

"I told you we should've explained years ago," snaps Rohan. I look at him expectantly. "Ria, I think you are my

23

blood but your mother's holds something more, which you inherited."

Camanor looks at my confusion. "The First-Born never fully explained what happened the day they defeated the Ebon Queen. Recently, they shared an interesting secret— when the Ebon First-Born died, her essence passed to one of the other people present. The Ebon essence now lives within Calla." He smiles at me. "And within you, as her daughter."

"Um. *I* didn't know that. Calla?" I say in shock and stand.

Four men in my life acting as guardians and fathers and not one ever told me the truth. My own *mother* lied to me.

"You were in danger from the First-Born who wanted all trace of the Ebon flight eradicated to prevent such destruction ever happening again," says Calla softly. "My bond to Luin kept me safe as the elders would not break such a union. But we couldn't risk what might happen to you if they discovered another person held a part of the Queen. Each time the elders visited to check whether the Ebon Queen's essence had influenced me, we pretended there's no child. Hence your visits to Devin at those times and why you now live with him. You are not the type of girl we could constrain within the court."

"Yet allowing her into the wide world made her more visible," says Camanor with a snort.

"The First-Born do not leave the dragon realms," says Luin sharply. "We believed she'd be safe and unnoticed."

He cocks his head. "Yes. But *I* do and have spent some time tracking down the Ebon essence we felt in the world. Calla, the other First-Born sensed that Lyrandra's soul faded within you over the years and weren't concerned. We can't say the same about Aurelia, can we? You're fortunate Talindra isn't angry enough to act on her... displeasure."

Rohan swears and glares at Galen. "I told you we

should've admitted to the elders once the dragon and human realms grew calmer. What if this causes discord?"

"Explain who you are, Camanor," interrupts Luin gruffly. "You have a name of power, but you are not a First-Born. Are you their general, come to take his enemy? Because you may be a dragon, but you face powerful people in this court."

Camanor's laughter fills the room with more animosity. "I am more diplomatic than stupid and do not wish to cause a rift between our races. But I'm not a general. I am an exarch —or if you'd like a title you'll understand, I'm a prince."

The only thing echoing now is silence that Luin breaks. "The First-Born have reinstated their courts and chosen exarchs? Is this not what caused problems the first time? Disharmony between the dragon flights?"

"Only because the Ebon took that disharmony and created a war. The other four flights desire nothing but peace." Camanor tips his chin. "We need to know if Aurelia is the Ebon flight presence we feel within the world, or if not whether an Ebon dragon survived."

"The Ebon Queen had no offspring," says Galen evenly. "And if Aurelia does contain the essence that's all. She is not a dragon nor capable of procreating with one."

"Nor interested *at all*," I put in.

I knew the story of Calla and my father's aiding in the Ebon Queen's death, but nobody ever mentioned my mother absorbing her power or essence or whatever Camanor calls it. More importantly, not that *I* have this essence.

Once the Ebon First-Born finished killing the other flights, she spent her life destroying elven and human lands. My father's Lumen elves were displaced and Ebon elves in her thrall took over their courts. Many, many people died as her decay spread.

The Ebon Queen wanted nothing but to engulf all lands and had no goodness within her.

And I have *her* in *me*? That's impossible.

Camanor sighs. "The First-Born requested that Aurelia come to them, and you know that they rarely make requests. If you ignore this, the elders will forcibly take her." He side-glances me and his lips twitch into a smile. "And Aurelia has discovered that I will not forcibly take her."

I scowl at him. "So, these dragons want to meet me?" I ask casually. "And then?"

"I'm unsure but they've promised not to kill Aurelia." Camanor addresses the others, blunt as usual. "As they kept their word once before, and you remain alive Calla."

"Mother?" I ask in horror and stand. "The dragons once chose to kill you?"

"Due to their fear I'd *become* the Ebon Queen. My relationship with Luin prevented their actions," she says. "My dragon soul is bonded to him."

Again, Camanor laughs. "Such outdated bullshit. 'Bonded' is merely a fancy name for 'don't touch my female or I'll rip your heart out', as if she's a possession."

"Calla is no possession," snarls Luin. "Exarch or not, do not address the Aureate Lady in that way."

"Well, at the time it saved your 'bonded's' life so be happy the First-Born have archaic ideas." Camanor stands too. "Ideas that the flights' princes are attempting to leave out of the current courts."

"Oh, stars," I mutter. "There are four of you? Are they all as unpleasant and arrogant?"

Camanor moves towards me, his silver eyes glinting as he bends at the waist to bring his mouth closer to my ear. "Do you feel that?" His sonorous voice sends a tremor through me, his breath sweet and warm. "Because if you do, there's enough female dragon essence inside you."

"Enough for what?" I attempt to retort but the words come out more breathlessly than I planned.

"Enough to find a dragon's cock irresistible, as you did last night." His face remains close and behind him I see Rohan about to step forward, but Leander places a hand on his chest.

Are all dragon's obsessed with the supposed wondrousness of their cocks?

Pulling my head away, I take Camanor's face and jerk his head to look at me. "Oh, good. Then I'll have a choice of four." Momentarily, he loses his cool expression and I move my face to whisper in the way he did. "Well, three because I definitely *don't* want your cock."

The look he gives me is filled with more than a dark annoyance as storm flares in his silver eyes adding an unnatural brightness. The weird energy I sensed around him last night intensifies.

I don't understand everything in his manner at this moment, but I do know one thing.

If we weren't in a room surrounded by my family, Camanor would demonstrate that he's finished humoring me, and I've stepped too far over a line.

CHAPTER 4

AURELIA

LUIN IS THE MOST VOCAL IN HIS RESISTANCE TO ME accompanying Camanor but then diplomacy was never his forte. The only person with sway over him is my mother and even that ends in a fight sometimes. Not physically, Luin would never touch his bonded in that way.

I had a long conversation with Calla alone and allowed myself to shed the tears with her that I refused to in front of the men, especially dragon-asshole. My anger at her had ebbed into feelings of betrayal but when she explained the threat to my life, I understood. I always had five fathers and, at the end of the day, who actually fathered me isn't the biggest issue.

The evil queen's essence and four dragon elders demanding I see them? Possible death? That's an issue.

I've no choice but to accompany Camanor to Reodian, the dragon city at the center of their lands. As a compromise, we've agreed that if I haven't returned within thirty days others will be sent to find me. We've warned Camanor that should anything untoward happen to me, there will be a severe crack in the accords between humans, elves, and dragons.

Seems I've moved from the assassin's daughter who might kill you to the woman with the essence of a dragon who could start a war.

As I prepare to leave, I join my mother again, this time in the personal gardens she spends so much time in, growing herbs and flowers for her tinctures and potions. She trained as an apothecary before her life turned upside down and landed her in the middle of a war but she still practices. Luckily for me, because I have a ready supply of healing salves and a particular herbal mix to stop accidentally falling with child. That's one she secretly supplies me because no father apart from Devin accepts that I've grown up, probably because when I last lived with them I was much younger.

Luin stands with her. I searched for him when I needed to say my goodbyes to the others and fully expected him to be one of the last to let me go. He was instrumental in rebirthing the dragon race and so Camanor at least showed *him* respect. After all, this Sapphire dragon wouldn't exist otherwise.

In fact, without the actions of my whole family, the First-Born would still be hidden, and the flights wouldn't exist. At the beginning of the dragon wars, all the First-Born essences were trapped—apart from the Ebon Queen's. My mother and fathers located the hidden eggs containing their souls and returned them to life. With the elders' help, Calla then killed the Ebon Queen.

Hopefully, they remember this when considering my fate.

Calla's long blonde hair hangs loose around her face today and she's pink-cheeked under the sun, picking and handing small bunches of herbs to Luin. I chuckle as I look at the tiny purple flowers in the man's huge hand as we talk.

"I remember Reodian as the city void of life, I'd very much wish to see the place filled with the dragons again," she comments.

Something between a rumble and a growl fills Luin's chest. "I guess 'daddy dragon' says no," I say.

"Aurelia." Calla shakes her head at my using the childish nickname I had for Luin, since I called all men 'daddy' until old enough to believe Devin is. They all were in some way, and all treated me as if they are. "And no, the last time I visited Reodian, the First-Born did not welcome my presence."

"Wonderful. They'll love me then," I say sarcastically.

"Camanor gave his assurances nothing will befall you. As he had ample opportunity to take and hurt you since he discovered your existence, then we must trust them." I snort at Calla's words, and she frowns. "Aurelia. You must take care."

"Sorry, mother." I chew my lip and lower my voice. "Disguising my nerves."

Luin continues to watch in silence, but his expression tells me he has plenty he'd like to say.

"Is this why you had no other children?" I ask her. "You worried you'd need to hide two from the dragons?"

She strokes my cheek. "I know you wanted a brother or sister, but yes, the chances another child may contain Ebon flight essence was too big a risk."

"Did you ever worry that I'd be like *her*?"

Dealing with the news my father isn't who I thought is hard. But discovering I contain the essence of a creature who decimated the human and elven realms and intended to spread her darkness and decay everywhere? Horrendous. I can only take comfort that Calla didn't succumb to the Queen's evil since she contains the essence too.

"No, Aurelia." My mother takes my head in both hands and kisses my forehead. "Never." She steps back.

"You have never felt the Ebon presence?" asks Luin in his deep voice.

I bite my lip. "Only that I'm inclined to robbing people and occasionally killing to defend my life. But I presumed this 'trait' came from Devin."

"You must promise me to never live the life he once did," Calla says softly.

"As an assassin?" I catch sight of Luin's eyes trained on me; I know how he feels about my killing people. "You think that may trigger something in me?"

"I don't know, but don't take the risk." Calla tips my chin. "Take care around the dragons. Perhaps rein in your attitude a little."

I chuckle. "I could never fight a dragon and win. Not physically anyway." She and Luin exchange a glance and he nods at her. My eyes narrow. "What?"

"What if this causes trouble?" says Calla to Luin in a hushed voice.

"If Aurelia must use this, then the trouble will already be caused," he replies.

"No. If they find this on her person."

"What is 'this'?" I ask.

Calla slips something from inside her sleeve, a small round vial containing a grayish-blue powder. My eyes widen. "Are you giving me something to harm dragons?"

"No. That will... incapacitate them," says Luin. "They won't suffer any ill effects."

I blink, heart speeding. "Calla is right. What if the dragons find me with this?"

"They won't know what you have. Tell them you use it for..." She glances at Luin. "Female reasons."

Luin clears his throat and straightens. "What female reasons? To prevent a child?"

I choke. "I'm not ever lying with a dragon." Luin's jaw hardens. "Not that it's *wrong*, just that I can't imagine wanting to."

"Don't underestimate the seductiveness of dragons, Aurelia," says Luin.

My mind flashes back to last night. Well, that wouldn't have ended with me fucking Camanor.

Honest.

"How do I incapacitate them? Throw it in their eyes?" I ask, and Calla frowns at my sarcasm.

"Put in their food or wine; it's tasteless. They can't shift with this in their body. Unfortunately, you'll need to protect yourself with a weapon for a more imminent threat," says Calla.

"If the dragons don't remove the assassin's daggers," I mutter and hold out my hand. "Dragons definitely won't know what this is?"

Luin shakes his head. "No. Not unless they see you with it."

"Hmm." Calla places the vial in my hand, and I shake the contents. "Any poison for my daggers?" She takes a sharp breath and I meet her worried eyes. "That was a joke."

"I've never given you poisons and never will."

Blowing air into my cheeks, I shove the vial in my boot. "If the Sapphire asshole or his other princely friends piss me off, I'll invite them to dinner."

CHAPTER 5

AURELIA

I RETURN TO WESTPORT WITH DEVIN, AND THE complaining dragon at our heels. Camanor could fly if he liked; people are accustomed to the sight now, but he won't leave my side. At least he's *respectful* when Devin is with me.

The decision to return to Westport isn't made because I'm to return home but because the port town edges the Southern Waters, which we must cross to reach the lands where the dragons' realm exists.

Camanor is pissed and I can't help my smugness that my family insisted I don't fly to Reodian if I don't wish too. The thought of Camanor as a dragon carrying me on his back scares me. He'd likely continue his attempts to intimidate me, and I bet he'd threaten to drop me for amusement.

The prince begrudgingly agrees but only if he stays with me. All the time. And he really does mean *all* the time. I've barely a moment's privacy without his smirking, arrogant face in mine.

I almost collide with him as I leave my room with my pack. "Stars! Did you think I'd climb through the window and run? Your constant watch becomes irritating, Cam."

Camanor rests against the wall in the narrow hallways and crosses his arms. "Fly. Then I won't need to shadow you until we arrive at Reodian. And I'd rather you called me 'My Prince'."

"No, Cam. I will not fly, and you are not 'My Prince'."

He huffs. "You prefer long journeys?"

"I rather fancy a trip across the seas." I hitch my pack higher. "Is that the issue? You become seasick?"

"No. I do not."

"Have you ever traveled by boat?"

"I've never needed to."

"Then how do you know, *My Prince*? I do hope you don't vomit on me." I pause. "You could fly and meet me there?"

"Hilarious, Lady Aurelia."

"Ria." I've never taken Galen's family title, nor do I intend to.

"Oh no, that won't do. You require a title, my little Ebon spitfire."

I glare. "Ria. I'll ignore anything else. And I am not Ebon."

He closes his eyes and sighs loudly. "You are determined to make our time together unpleasant."

"But you told me that time ends when we reach Reodian." He nods. "What happens to me there?"

"That's the First-Borns' decision." Cam pulls himself from the wall again. "Don't look horrified. You've little choice. Now we know who you are, until you meet the elders, they'll keep searching. I doubt they'll hurt you—we can't have your essence escaping elsewhere if you die."

"Excuse me?" My voice rises in pitch.

"Your dragon father wouldn't allow you to come with me otherwise. He understands the danger."

I grip the strap of my pack, remembering how pissed I was when Luin agreed, even knowing the First-Born wanted to harm my mother for containing a dragon soul.

"I could have Luin's dragon essence, not Ebon," I suggest. "My mother did lie with him at the same time as my father."

"At the same time?" Cam mocks shock. "Humans fuck in multiples too? I thought only elves took part in such *filthy* practices."

"Not dragons?" I ask. "How unusual since you seem the most depraved of all."

He pushes his tongue against a sharp canine and smirks. "Well, some. Not everybody follows traditions, Aurelia."

The stairs creak, and Devin appears at the top. As with most elves, he's older than the twenty-something he looks but today Devin's strained expression ages him.

"Devin. Aurelia believes she has Luin's essence since Calla fucked him. Tell her that you sense the Ebon too."

"Your attitude disgusts me, Camanor," snaps Devin. "I am increasingly worried about allowing Ria to accompany you. You talk of the High Lady of the Aureate Court with rudeness and disdain; I can't believe that you care for diplomacy—and that makes Ria unsafe."

"I don't wish her harm," says Cam. "Neither do the First-Born. It's not my fault you don't understand the ways of dragons."

"Yet you won't allow me to accompany you," he says.

Cam gestures at me. "Aurelia?"

"I'm the one who wishes to travel unaccompanied, Devin," I reply and refuse to break my gaze when he looks on me in shock. "If I am what they fear, I can defend myself. If I'm not, they'll no doubt grow bored with me." Cam laughs in his annoying, condescending way and Devin straightens, eyes narrowing. "And I don't wish *you* to be the one to cause the diplomatic problem by attacking this arrogant asshole halfway to Reodian."

I KNOW THE SHIP'S CAPTAIN WELL AND HE'S HAPPY TO TAKE me across the Waters but does not greet Cam with a warm welcome.

Instead, Fin's tanned face is plastered with a scowl. The ship's captain looks as wild as the seas he navigates with dark scruff covering his cheeks and chin, unruly curls captured in a ponytail where strands escape and fall around his face. He's dressed in black trousers that accentuate his broad figure, his white shirtsleeves rolled up, showing strong forearms and the edge of a dark tattoo on his right. As a child, I fancied he was a pirate for the sole reason he had gold hoops in his ears.

"Why are you bringing a dragon onto my ship?" he asks me, as if Cam isn't looming over us both. "You asked for passage to Lightpoint Harbor but didn't mention your *companion*."

"We're traveling to Reodian for an audience with the First-Born," I reply and Fin's eyes narrow to slits. As a close friend of Devin's, he knows of my family's links to the dragons—although not everything. *Obviously.* "My only other option is to fly with him, Fin," I say. "I don't want to fly across the Waters with a dragon and Cam won't leave me alone, so he is traveling with me."

"Fly?" Fin arches a brow. "I understand your concern."

Cam makes a sound somewhere between a growl and a laugh. "Because I might drop her?"

Fin runs a tongue along his teeth and takes a long look at Cam. "While you are on my ship, you show Ria respect."

"And why presume I will not?"

"Because you're a dragon." This time, Cam definitely growls but Fin dismisses him and looks to me. "Ria, you may dine with me tonight."

"You do not extend your hospitality to her companion?" asks Cam and I silently will Fin to soften his attitude.

I sigh. "Please invite Cam, Fin, otherwise he'll be in a bad mood and even more unbearable."

Fin's eyes narrow. "Dragon, I would like to speak to Ria alone for a few moments. You can check out your lodgings for tonight, although I'm sure they're not what you're accustomed to."

"Can I not take the captain's bed?" he asks, as if Fin suggested he sleep in a pigsty. "For a price. I have plenty of gold."

"No, Ria will sleep in my bed," says Fin.

"What?" Cam's silver eyes flare.

I bite my lip to hide a smile and look the other way. Fin always allows me his bed, but never with him beside me—he's the same age as my human fathers and has known me since I was a small child.

"What's wrong?" I ask him. "Jealous?"

I'm heavily sarcastic but Cam doesn't reply, instead his huge frame disappears through the hatch leading below deck.

"You don't need to give me your bed, Fin," I say.

"I don't trust dragons. I'm expecting him to steal from my cargo, but he won't lay a finger on you," says Fin and touches my cheek. "Why are you traveling with him, you're evidently not friends?"

"Long story." I flash him a smile. "Devin knows where I'm going; I'm not in danger." I hope.

A blue-haired head re-appears, and Cam hauls himself upwards. "I would barely fit in that... whatever you call the excuse for a bed."

"Bunk," says Fin. "Sleep on the floor if you prefer."

A muscle twitches in his jaw. "I'd prefer not to. I'll stay awake."

"All night?" I frown.

He steps forward and looks down. "Dragons are not men, Aurelia. We're not weakened by their need for constant rest and food."

"Well, don't worry yourself that I'll jump overboard and swim away. I'm perfectly safe in Fin's bed." Again, the displeased look. I bite back a smile. "Why is that an issue?"

"I'm not annoyed that you're sleeping in Fin's bed, only that I would like to be the one who does."

My eyes widen. "Really? I'm not sure that Fin fucks dragons and if he did, I can assure you he wouldn't choose a male."

Fin chuckles but the darkness of Cam's expression causes me to take a small step backwards. "How amusing, Aurelia."

I turn away. I should heed Calla's words and not taunt this man. "Fin. Do you need any aid in preparing the ship for voyage?"

CHAPTER 6

AURELIA

FROM MY VANTAGE POINT IN THE RIGGING, I CAN SEE CAM watching me, his gaze unwavering, and my scalp prickles. Either side of us, other boats are docked, merchant ships half the size of this one and others dwarfing Fin's. There's a second crew member who pays little attention to me or Cam, no doubt accustomed to unusual clients traveling with the ship. The shaven haired man is new and young, and Fin tells me he's an apprentice who knows how to keep his mouth shut to keep his job.

Late afternoon, Westport authorities arrived to inspect the cargo. Fin's known for shipping more 'exotic' items that may or may not be legally carried, but the two stocky men in their smart port authority uniform find nothing. They barely glance at Cam, now sitting on deck, half-hidden by his cloak, but they look at me with curiosity.

I wave as they leave and then return to the ropes.

"You should stop before the sun sets," Cam calls now.

The sky fills with magentas and light pink amongst the burnt orange stretched across the horizon, the beautiful sunset above the cobbled Westport streets. The skies smile down on our planned voyage, promising calm. I peer down at where Cam stands again, arms tightly crossed over his expansive chest. I can only see the edge of his face beneath the hood but imagine his expression is as sour or haughty as ever.

"Climb down, in case you fall," he adds.

"Don't worry your pretty head, Cam," I call down. "I've had plenty of practice. And you can stop the constant supervision; I'm not leaving the ship."

"Perhaps I like the view," he comments. "Your ass looks good from this angle."

I don't dignify him with a response and turn my back again.

ONLY WHEN FIN APPEARS AND OFFERS US SUPPER, DO I clamber back down. To be honest, I long since finished the rigging and if Cam knew anything about ships, he'd realize there's no longer any point in my staying up here now we've set sail.

I just prefer to keep out of his way.

The captain's round table is lain with cured meats and boiled vegetables on wooden plates beside silver cups and welcome bottles of rum. The three of us sit in a semi-circle with me opposite Fin, and Cam to my left, far enough away not to touch.

The Sapphire Prince touches nothing as he watches us eat. If this is distasteful to him, what is royal dragon food like? I'd ask but prefer to keep conversation to what's necessary. His size and presence fills the galley, and he's dispensed with his cloak giving a display of power in his massive shoulders and broader than human chest. I stare at him as I sip the rough dark rum and he gives me a lazy smile.

"Do you often stare at men as if you'd prefer them for dinner?" he asks

"I'm imagining you as a dragon," I reply. "That's all."

"And if we flew, you'd see what one looked like," he says pointedly.

"One of my fathers is a dragon, remember? I've seen him fly plenty of times." I return to my food.

"Well then, I'm happy to show you the whole of my *unshifted* form, Aurelia. Just ask."

That deep tone sends an involuntary shiver through at my body's memory of that form pressed against me. "Thanks, but no thanks."

He shrugs. "Pour me a drink."

I look to Fin, unsure who he's addressing, and the captain shoves a bottle towards him. "Pour your own, dragon."

With a noise of displeasure, Cam fills his cup to the brim and sniffs before taking a mouthful. His face pulls into disgust and he gags. "Gods, how do you consume such an awful wine?"

"Rum," I correct. Admittedly, Fin saves his decent rum for himself, and guests are served the rough as guts variety. "Does the trick on cold nights."

"Luckily you have a warm bed too," he says.

"Fin's?" I can't resist touching on something that annoys Cam.

Fin winks at me and tears a piece of meat with his teeth.

The atmosphere settles as Fin and I consume more rum, and the captain quizzes Cam on how dragons navigate when flying. Fin then begins to nose into dragon affairs and what he might sell them. Too lulled by the good meal and rum in my body, and not wanting to sleep yet, I slip away for some air.

The black sea is calm tonight, although I'd like to know how Cam would've fared on a rougher voyage. I've looked over this deck on journeys where the waves pounded the boat many times and never experienced sickness. I'd gripped on, thrilled by the danger held inside the water below and once stood beneath a storm, shivering as I watched the lit clouds, waiting for lightning to strike the deck.

That never happened, and I never found myself tipped into the churning waters. Luckily, since I once glimpsed the sharp-toothed fish, shocked they're as large as a man.

Tonight, my thoughts are only on the recent news about my heritage. Is that the attraction to storms? The thrill of anything dangerous? I've dreamed things in the past that would wake me up drenched in sweat but could never remember what I'd seen, only that a dread feeling seeped through my bones. Darkness lingered in the room, swallowing me, and then I'd wake a second time, realizing that was part of the dream too.

Now, I'm more disturbed by those occasions—is this the Ebon inside me?

An almost full moon lights the calm seas, like a rippling pathway between us and the horizon. Galen can use the moon for spells though rarely calls on the goddess's power. Although once, he showed me how he could persuade the full moon to create a *real* solid pathway across the waters that I ran along, giggling.

A cloud obscures the moon, and then the sea brightens again but moments later the same thing happens. Shielding my eyes, I look upwards; the skies were clear minutes ago. A shape high above could be seabird, but none would fly that high and if they did, would not look so large. The giant bird crosses the moon and I strain my eyes.

Dragon.

Dragons in flight aren't an unusual sight these days but I'll never stop my fascination how something so unnatural can also be a man or woman. Idly, I wonder if I could fly then burst into laughter at myself. Calla can't. As I stand with a new breeze whipping my hair, the shape dips down, circling the boat, uncomfortably like a bird of prey, the space shrinking as the creature moves slower and closer.

Stars.

This is not good.

One reason for dragons' bad reputation? They're also huge pirates and target ships whose captains could never ask for help from authorities. Those merchants who'd draw attention to their dodgy choice of cargo if they sought assistance.

Like Fin.

Fuck.

The dragon moves low enough that the buttery yellow light shines across dark scales. Which flight? I'm not bothered that the moonlight doesn't reveal the dragon's color, only that he's close enough for me to *see* scales. This dragon is half the length of the ship and I swear about to land.

Warn Fin.

I trip over my feet as I make towards the hatch, and my hair blows into my face as the slow sound of flapping, leathery wings grows uncomfortably close. Something akin to hands curl around either side of my waist, and I'm too stunned to make a noise as my feet lift from the deck. By the time I find my voice and scream out I may as well be a seagull screeching into the night.

CHAPTER 7

AURELIA

DAZED WITH SHOCK, I PLACE MY HANDS ON WHATEVER
holds me, even though the answer is fucking obvious.

Taloned paws.

Luin carried me this way a few times, and I'd shriek and
laugh as he swooped around. Leander and Galen would read
to me, others taught me to fight or use weapons. My dragon
father played our game that terrified my mother, but I loved
flying in his paws more than the normal way—riding on his
back.

Yes, I've experienced the strong grip around my body
before, legs dangling as I clung onto Luin's legs, but a few
meters off the ground, not so high that the ship disappears
from view.

Usually, if someone I don't like or know holds my body, I
reward them with a dagger to the limb. I've one sheathed to
my thigh and always carry a smaller second weapon, usually in
my boot, as today. But unless I want to be dropped into the

seas below, I've no choice but to plan what to do when he puts me down.

I swear the asshole swoops up and down to make me shriek, even though his grip is tight enough I feel the tips of claws in my side. The shock that spiked my body when he lifted me from the boat is replaced by heart-thumping, mind-addling terror.

What the fuck will this dragon to do to me?

My face stings from the dragon flying at high speed through the cool night, limbs becoming numb. I'm only wearing a thin, long-sleeved tunic and pants, since I left my cloak inside the ship.

Some minutes later, tiny lights from a town at the edge of the Southern Waters appear, multiplying as the dragon pulls us closer. We fly across the port town with streets too narrow for a dragon to land and I slap at his paws.

"Do you know how fucking cold I'm getting from dangling in the air like this?" The steady, beats slow a little but he or she doesn't speak as my heart continues to pound. "I can't fly like this, you bastard. You're hurting me."

Suddenly, Cam's intent supervision over the last two days doesn't feel as invasive—was he watching me to stop this happening?

As we glide over the buildings at the edge of the town, the lights retreat in the distance again, and the dragon flies lower and lower until a pathway appears below, one leading from the port into the land between the town and the next. I hope he slows down, so I don't break my legs when we land.

He doesn't slow down. Oh no—the bastard releases my waist and I fall from the height of a two story building, curling up and landing on dirt and grass, gasping as air knocks from me at the impact. My racing heart doesn't slow as I turn onto my back and try to stand, scanning the skies for the dragon.

Nothing.

Attempting to fill my painfully empty lungs with air, I drag myself upright and continue to search above for any sign of him.

If the dragon isn't flying any longer, that means he's on the ground somewhere.

Looking for me.

And I'm standing in the moonlight.

I tear into the wooded area to my left, struggling to navigate the closely packed trees, scratching my legs on low-lying bushes as I allow the dark to take me. If he's as big as Cam as a man, this dragon won't fit through this undergrowth easily in his male form.

No. He'll probably barge right through.

Shit. What if he's still shifted?

And what the fuck is happening?

Locating a thick trunk, I move into the darkest place I can find where the canopies bend together to block out the light. Moss on the tree touches my forehead as I rest and take more ragged breaths.

Calm. Focus. This isn't the first time I've hidden in woods —either as the pursuer or the pursued. I lean down, carefully withdraw the blade from its sheath.

I've the advantage that I'm light-footed when a dragon certainly isn't. I always knew when Luin searched for me, although part of the stomping was no doubt his perpetual bad mood.

Which town did we fly over? Lightpoint Harbor, I think, as the dragon only flew for a few minutes, and I saw ships docked. I could make my way there since I know the place and also a few of the residents, although I'd rather avoid some of them.

The road I'm on must be the one leading inland to a larger town, but the lands where the dragon city flies above aren't my king's realm and my position as a High Lady's daughter means nothing.

I rub my cold cheek. Head to the harbor and wait for passage back to Westport? As I listen over my breathing for any sounds in the woods around—dragon or animal—I picture Fin's panic when he discovers I'm missing. I never alerted Fin and unless he heard my scream high in the air. He might believe I fell overboard.

And Cam. Will *he* think I went against my promise not to escape?

Seriously, about now I wish I'd invited Cam into Fin's cabin and kept him close rather than walked on deck. Just because one dragon was semi-nice to me doesn't mean another will be. What if I've injured or dispatched someone this dragon knows and that's the reason for the less than kind abduction? Searching my murky past, I can't remember harming a dragon although I've stolen from one.

Stolen. Maybe that's why he took me—dragons don't take kindly to people separating them from their possessions.

The thought pains me, but at this moment I hope Cam resumes his search for me.

I've spent time in these parts but not so much in the woods, although I know they line the way to town before thinning out a short distance before the streets crowd with houses and shops. So, there's only a short distance where I'll be visible if I manage to stay inside the woods. If I can navigate the right direction in the bloody dark.

Reassured there's nobody around unless a dragon suddenly can sneak, I begin to edge my way through the trees, sticking to the thickest parts and ignoring the fresh scratches from thorny bushes that I'm forced to push out of my way. Wolves and whatever monstrosities the Ebon elves once created don't live in this part of the realm but I'm still wary what might. Plus, I've had unpleasant encounters with rabbit traps before and want to avoid those too.

A short time trudging later and I almost step into a small clearing until a shape in the shadows arrests me. This time the moonlight picks out the red in a dark-clothed man's hair and he matches Cam in size.

A Ruby flight dragon. I immediately step back before he notices my presence.

He's resting a shoulder against a tree and picking at his nails with partial claws on the other hand, as if waiting for an acquaintance who's late to a meeting. Gritting my teeth, I size up my surroundings. A dragon's acute hearing would sense me soon, if not my smell, so I begin to edge into a position I can attack from.

The dragon remains still. If this isn't the one who ripped me from the ship, then Ruby dragons enjoy loitering in the middle of quiet woods, which doesn't seem likely to me.

Concentrate. Be swift.

I bolt from the trees then collide my knee with the back of his, causing him to stumble but not go down as a man would. With claws digging into the bark to stay upright, the dragon turns to face me, red eyes glinting in the dark, but I have the tip of my blade at his neck before he can properly react. As he moves to seize me, I press the blade harder until it pierces his skin.

He swears at me. "I'll break your fucking arm before you can do any damage."

"Try me."

"Try *me*." His bared teeth gleam.

"I presume that if you took me from the ship alive, you've a reason *not* to kill me," I retort.

"Who said anything about killing you?" His huge hand curls around my slender wrist. "Last chance, girl. Drop your weapon or I'll snap your bones."

"How would the First-Born feel if you took them damaged goods?" I hiss as he squeezes, and I pierce his skin further.

He falters. "First-Born? How do you know I want to take you to them?"

"You're not the first dragon who's 'found' me recently." I stumble as he shoves me to one side and drags a hand through his hair.

"What the fuck? Who found you first?" he snarls.

"Uh. The dragon on the ship you so charmingly abducted me from."

"Who?" he demands. "Luc? Cam?"

Cool trickles through my blood. "Exactly *how* many dragons are chasing me?"

"The four flights' exarchs. Who found you?" he snaps again. "Fucking Cam, I'll wager. I knew he'd get to you first."

"First?" I swallow. "Are you fighting over me?"

The dragon takes a disdainful look over my figure. "Why hasn't he taken you back to Reodian yet? Surely if you don't cooperate, Cam can break you if he needs to. You're no match for a dragon."

"What?" A twig snaps as I step back. "Were you serious about breaking my bones?"

His high brow dips, and he leans forward, face almost touching my head as he sniffs. "Cam. I can smell him on you."

"He hasn't touched me for a couple of days."

"Aha. He seduced you? Why am I not surprised." The man sweeps a gaze along me again. "Although why dragons fuck humans, I have no idea. I'm surprised *he* didn't snap your bones while you did. You must be stronger than you look."

"I am, but I didn't fuck your dragon friend."

The man waves a dismissive hand. "Like I care. I have you in my possession now, so he's lost."

49

Possession. I gape as fury rolls through my veins. "*Lost?* Am I part of a fucking game?"

"Not exactly but we are in competition." As he smirks at my horror, I take another step back.

"I'm not going with you."

His laugh fills the night. "Yes, you are."

The asshole who hasn't introduced himself places a palm on the tree and leans against it. I was correct about the 'all dragons are smug, arrogant bastards' theory. "Who are you?"

"Velanor. Ruby exarch." He flicks his tongue against his top teeth. "A pleasure to meet you, Aurelia." His voice drips with sarcasm.

"That pleasure is not mutual. Do you not realize how dangerous flying high with me in your paws was?" I snap.

"Yes, which is why you'll travel on my back the rest of the way to Reodian."

"Wrong."

"You want me to carry you in the same manner?" He tips his head. "Strange creature."

"You can't shift here," I tell him. "There isn't enough room."

"We can walk to the pathway." He smiles. "I know you won't be stupid enough to run. I'm faster than you."

"Uh huh," I reply and slam my dagger into the hand he's resting on the trunk.

Velanor's roar echoes in my ears as I sprint from the clearing and into the trees, praying that even though he has more strength, that he isn't as nimble as I am.

And that his hand attached to the trunk might give me some extra time.

Honestly, I'm not having a great night.

CHAPTER 8

AURELIA

AURELIA. THE CHANCES YOU'LL OUTRUN A DRAGON PRINCE ARE slim to none, particularly one whose hand you stabbed and neck you cut.

I stumble to a halt as the trees thin, allowing light to filter through and show a clearer route towards the pathway. Rubbing my mouth, I edge forward to gauge how far to the town from here.

But my adrenaline-filled blood sinks into my boots.

The dragon sits in the middle of the roadway, leaning back, palms behind him on the ground.

Shit.

With a sigh, I trudge out of the tree line. Velanor doesn't stand, only regards me across the small distance between us.

"I've killed people for less than that," he says evenly as he holds up a bloodied hand.

This chokes me, but I say, "Sorry. I was scared."

He seems to consider my words as he stands and produces

my weapon from beneath his cloak. "We leave, or I *will* hurt you."

"Don't take me yet," I blurt. "Let me rest first."

He scoffs. "Are you serious? And risk one of the others finding you?"

The famous dragon pride might help me here. I nod at his hand. "How long until that heals? Luin heals faster than a man."

"Luin? Oh. Your mother's dragon." He peers at the wound. "A few hours."

Still at a distance, I eye my dagger, bloodied at the tip. "You don't want anyone to see how a pathetic human managed to injure you. How embarrassing." He snarls at me. "Cam is on a ship or looking for me with no clue where I've gone—are the others close by?"

"No idea."

"Let me rest a few hours—and until you lose your embarrassing injury. Then I'll agree to go quietly."

Velanor flicks his tongue against a canine. "No. Another could snatch you."

"Like you did?" I arch a brow and wave a hand around. "Out in the open or at sea, yes. At an inn? Less likely if you're by my side. Cam was smart about that until I walked on deck alone."

Velanor's fingers rub across the puncture wound on his hand. "And if I allow this, you will tell the First-Born that I located you first?"

"Gods. You're rather deceitful as a race. Cam won't like that."

He shrugs. "He shouldn't have been so *nice*."

I tip my head up. The stars shine brighter in the clear sky and the realization that I never knew what I'm truly dealing with returns. Cam was *nice* to me? Hmm. "Why do the First-

Born want me? Cam told me some of the story but apparently not all."

"Don't know. Don't care, Ebon bitch."

I choke. "How lovely. I guess I have my answer."

Boots kick up dirt as he strides forward and stares down; I catch my breath at the disgust in his eyes. "The Ruby flight suffered the most at the hands of the Ebon. They tortured the men. Killed women and children for sport. Now we're reborn, there is no *fucking* way any creature with Ebon essence inside can stay loose in the world."

My chest tightens in panic. "I'm not Ebon, Velanor."

"Yet you are." He tips his chin. "The First-Born won't kill you and release that essence into the ether, but you need dealing with."

"By you?" I ask hoarsely.

Long fingers curl around my neck, just below my chin and his mouth moves closer to my face. "You'd better pray not."

Fear at a level I've never experienced before screams through me. He threatened to break my arm moments after we met and I'm now certain he would crush me if he had an excuse.

Or permission.

What if the prize for this so-called competition is *me*?

If I can delay this enough for either Cam to find me or to escape from Velanor, that's a better outcome than if this dragon snatches me now.

Who knows? Maybe he's hungry, and I can add a little something to his meal?

———

ALTHOUGH MY COMMENT ABOUT EMBARRASSING INJURIES BY a human was a shot in the dark, pride *is* important to this creature. Also, fortunately, dragon princes don't favor roughing a night in the woods and he agrees to finding a place to stay. *If* I stay within his sight at all times and refuse to go with any other dragon, should one find me.

I'm buoyed by the idea but also carry a sinking feeling—Velanor wouldn't allow this if he believed another dragon were close enough to locate me. How far across the realms are they searching for me? Cam must've figured out where I am before the others, and I bet he didn't tell anybody where he traveled to.

And how *long* have they searched for the Ebon?

Even late at night, people wander Lightpoint's streets; the ones stupid enough to risk attack and the ones who'll accost them. "Shit. I wish I had a cloak," I mutter as my head remains bowed. "There're people I'd rather not see."

He snorts. "And they'd fight a dragon in order to harm you? No man would succeed. Or woman, Aurelia."

I clench my teeth because he's correct.

The Sailors Arms is closest to the edge of town and fortunately I'm on good terms with the innkeeper, an old friend of Devin's who has 'retired' from his original employment for a less risky job. Seb bears the scars of his past work on his face and arms. Devin's unmarked skin is another reason people believe he's Switfblade, the untouchable assassin.

And this encourages them not to upset him by harming his daughter. Shame that doesn't extend to dragons.

Another perfect thing about the Sailors Arms? Dingy. Makes the place popular with low lives, but thief's honor and all that. Too many sweaty sailors are jammed in amongst the townsfolk, filling the space with raucousness and stench as they sit around the scratched tables gambling with dice. Someone is a sore loser because there's a fight at one end of the tavern that's already led to smashed bottles.

Seb whose slender frame is deceptively strong, threatens

to throw them onto the street and I pause with Velanor beside me as I wait for him to cross back to the bar.

"Gods," mutters Velanor. "Is this how humans live?"

"You don't get out much then?" I ask lightly.

He sneers. "I don't leave my court or Reodian often and certainly keep away from humans. This confirms why."

A swarthy man, eyes awash with alcohol, stares at Velanor from across the nearest table. He nudges the shaggy-haired one beside him, who lifts his head from the table and blinks before setting it back down. The staring man unsteadily stands and uses the table to guide himself around.

I smell him before he reaches us, and he sways slightly as he peers at Velanor. "Never seen a red one."

Velanor doesn't respond. Even in the poor light, he's clearly a Ruby dragon, and the intensity of the red eyes adds more menace to his animosity. He resembles Cam a lot, and although his dour face replaces Cam's arrogant smile, he has the same sharp features and strong jaw.

The drunk man blinks at me. "What's a pretty thing doing in this hole?"

I narrow my eyes. "Ask Seb."

"Huh? You a whore? Work here?"

Velanor snarls. "Step away."

Confused by his sudden chivalry, I nudge Velanor. "I'm perfectly able to take care of myself."

"I do *not* keep company with whores. She is an... acquaintance," he snaps at the man then points at Seb. "Aurelia, tell that other man to find you a room."

"Staying?" The man cocks a brow and slides his tongue around his lips. "If you don't like the company of dragons, join us."

He chokes out when Velanor seizes him around the throat and lifts him from the sticky tavern floor. "The girl does not leave my sight."

Shit. I was lucky to avoid *that* earlier. The man's eyes bulge and Velanor pauses to let his words register then places the man's feet back on the floor.

Nobody else pays any attention, apart from Seb who ambles over. He frowns at me, and I swear he has a new scar across his high forehead, partially hidden by his long black hair. "Ria? Why are you in these parts?" Without waiting for an answer, he regards Velanor. "Interesting company. I didn't think you liked their kind."

I shrug. "The unfortunate man needs my help. How could I refuse?"

My capacity to make this man growl continues to amuse me. "I am not unfortunate, but you will be if you don't shut your mouth."

Seb's eyes slide to me, and he opens his mouth to defend me, but I shake my head. "Don't worry. He's soft-hearted under all his bluff. Likes to think he's the big man in charge." I lower my voice. "So, I let him."

"If you don't behave, I may change my mind about staying, Aurelia," Velanor retorts.

I bite back more I'd like to say. "Seb. I need a room and some supper. As does my friend."

Seb sucks on his teeth and looks between us. "Very well. Find a table."

I've no appetite, having eaten before this asshole snatched me, but ask for stew and ale. Two bowls. Two cups. One jug. Locating a small table, I perch on a stool as Velanor struggles to fit on his.

His reaction to the food matches Cam's and I keep an eye on him as I slide the vial from inside my boot. Unfortunately, his eyes remain wholly on me. "Try some ale. Experience human culinary delights."

"Eat and sleep," he retorts. "You have until sunrise."

But I slosh the ale into his cup anyway.

Nearby, someone spoiling for a fight makes a loud, rude comment about dragons. Vel twists around in his seat and glares at them, demonstrating his teeth and claws. In the moments before he turns back, I sprinkle a small amount of powder into his ale.

Velanor's eyes glow blood red as he mutters something dark in his language, so I push the mug to him. "At least try."

Huffing, he drinks. My heart skips when I'm convinced Velanor is about to spit the mouthful out, his eyes look that pained, but instead he swallows and pushes the mug away. Half empty. How much powder to subdue him? I only used half in case I needed more later. And how long will this work for if I'm successful?

I tap my fingers on the wood and look out of the grimy window—or attempt to. Velanor sits stiffly and quietly.

"You're not very talkative," I comment and nibble potato from the salty stew.

"I have little to say."

I roll my eyes. "I thought *Cam* was rude, but he's charming compared to you. Are the other flights' princes more or less nasty than you?"

His strange eyes turn to mine. "Cam might be friendlier due to your relationship to Luinor. My Emerald friend Luc? I don't know. He's *soft-hearted* with our kind. Possibly not you. As for Eli..." He shrugs.

"But they'd also snatch me given the chance." Velanor nods as if his last words took all his effort. "Is this pursuit a game or is there a purpose?" He yawns. "Why are all four princes pursuing me?"

"Because we were instructed," he says tersely.

"Cam didn't mention anybody else sought me. He even came to the Aureate Court to meet my family and assure them I'll be well."

"Clever bastard." Velanor half-smiles. "Shame he's lost the challenge now."

"Considering he lied to me, I don't care." I swallow. "Or should I? What do you win?"

"Win? Honor, I imagine."

"You *imagine*? That's why you're pursuing a woman around the realms?"

Velanor glares. "The First-Born are not to be questioned and their instructions followed at all times. Without them, the flights would not exist."

"Without my mother you mean," I mutter.

"What did you say?"

"I bet you don't know the full story about how the First-Born returned to the world."

"The fairy tales about humans and noble journeys with the flights' essences? We believe the First-Borns' version."

"Which is?"

He sucks on his teeth. "Irrelevant to you."

This time, I mutter expletives under my breath. Velanor yawns a second time. Or third? I hastily drain my mug. "Right. I'm tired."

"Good. I'm fed up with your talking." He rises and I scowl before doing the same.

Velanor stands behind me as Seb slides a key across the bar, attached to a square lump of wood. "We're full. Take that one."

The ale-soaked wood is damp in my hand. "Full? But this *is* a room?"

"Very top." He roves a gaze over Velanor. "If you're not friendly, you soon will be."

"What does that mean?" I'm jostled by a skinny man beside me who's rewarded with a shove from Velanor. "Vel. A human won't take me. Stop worrying."

"That is not a name for you to use. You call me Velanor."

With a sigh, I move back and navigate my way through the bodies and through a door at the rear of the inn. To the left, rickety stairs lead upwards, illuminated by a single lantern that barely lights the way.

Hand on the daubed wall to guide me, I climb the steps. We reach one narrow hallway where shrieks and laughter come from behind doors, then continue up the stairs until we reach a tiny space beneath with a slanted ceiling.

Attics.

Gods, no. I've stayed here before and I know what to expect.

CHAPTER 9

AURELIA

Fumbling to unlock the door, I shove it open and gesture into the room for Velanor to walk first. He ducks down and hits his shins on the edge of a bed.

"What is this?" he snaps.

The bed is jammed against one wall, the roof slanted to the degree that the dragon can only stand in one end of the room, close to the bed's head. The ragged blankets are folded onto the end of a lumpy mattress with two flat pillows. The only spare space at the foot of the bed is stacked with wooden crates containing who knows what.

"Sleep on the floor."

He stares at the scratched floorboards. "There isn't any room."

"I'm not getting into a bed with you," I retort. "Sleep outside."

"I have no desire to share a bed with you. You'd probably

shiv me in my sleep," he bites back. "And certainly not *that* bed. A child couldn't lie in there and no man would want to."

"Then what? Stand in the corner all night?" I shake my head and plop my backside onto the bed. The room smells awful and black mold smears the edge of the ceiling. "I'd rather not sleep with you nearby either. You might break my arm."

He sneers and lifts up his hand. "I owe you an injury."

I tense and debate whether to push past him through the doorway. Did I need the whole vial to incapacitate him?

"Why did I listen to your pathetic pleas?" he mutters.

"Because you're too proud." I arch a brow.

Alone with Cam in the Westport house held an odd energy—something I sense from both dragons—and in this smaller room that's more intense. Cam's energy switched on a sexually charged encounter but there's no way I want to touch this man. Velanor scares me because his power simmers with dislike bordering on hatred, as if I'm the one responsible for everything the Ebon Queen did.

"Does that mean you're remaining in the room?" I ask as he closes the door.

"Intuitive. Give me your dagger." He holds his massive hand out. "Otherwise, I'll drag you outside and fly you to Reodian."

"You have my dagger."

"You never carry more than one?"

I suck on my teeth. "Sometimes."

"Now?" The angry power rolls from him and convinced he'll frisk me if I don't, I pull the dagger from my boot and toss it onto the bed.

Velanor studies the blade for a moment before sliding it into his own boot.

"When you shift, you'd better not lose that," I retort.

He ignores me. "Sleep if you're tired. Isn't that the reason we're here?"

"And you won't touch me?"

"No. I don't like you, but I won't assault you in that way." He flicks a gaze along me. "Nor do I wish to. Wasn't Cam enough for you?"

"You *will* stand in the corner all night?" I ask. I'm not confirming or denying his veiled question.

"Perhaps."

As he crosses his arms and leans against the wall, my mouth parches at the sight of the puncture wound on his pale skin. That's enough reason to believe the man can hold his temper, which is pretty impressive for a dragon.

Lying in the bed, I shuffle as far across the mattress as I can without pressing my face onto the wall, pulling a musty smelling blanket over me. There's no possibility I'll sleep. *Please let my mother's herbs work.*

And then? I'll find somewhere else to hide. Cross back over the seas. Return to the Aureate court.

But my plans are doomed to failure; I can't outrun four dragons. Hopefully Cam will find me, or the one Velanor thought would be kinder.

I'm a fucking game. My jaw clenches. Cam might be a nicer dragon than this one, but he tricked my family into believing I'll be safe.

At least *he* knows I've a deal to return safely after thirty days.

The mattress sinks and I almost roll into the dragon as his weight pulls that side of the bed downward. I glance over my shoulder at a broad back, momentarily impressed by the sheer muscle, every knot straining against that gray tunic. Is he feeling the powder's effects because his head is in his hands?

"How strong is this 'ale' you gave me," he mutters and steadies himself with one hand on the mattress.

Yes.

I swiftly turn my back and close my eyes, deepening my breathing. Swearing, Velanor lies beside me, swallowing up almost the entire bed.

My arm touches his, and like Cam, he's unnaturally warm. Whatever aura these creatures surround themselves with wraps around me. There's something about powerfully built men that attracts me—I'm more likely to be distracted by a man's corded forearms than the rest of him and the one beside me, I hate to say, is magnificent. I close my eyes and inhale common sense. Unfortunately, I breathe in Velanor's scent and not sense, although the deep and masculine smell is preferable to the moldy one.

Again, unfortunately, appealing.

Am I naturally attracted to these creatures because I contain their essence? Because the 'situation' with Cam hinted I am.

Light shines through the small skylight window above and as Vel's breaths slow, I shift again and look at his face. I continue my gazing until I'm satisfied that he's either unconscious or asleep and wriggle to sit, which presents me with a problem.

To leave the bed, I'll need to climb over him, which won't be easy considering how close the sloped ceiling is to my head. My eyes drift along Vel's wide thigh towards the boot halfway up his calf. My dagger is in his left which I can only reach once I'm on the other side of him.

Fuck.

Kneeling with my head bowed so I don't hit the ceiling, I weigh up what to do. Is he definitely asleep or unconscious? Watching and waiting, I steel myself. He hasn't budged an inch nor has the rhythmic movements from his breathing stopped.

Cautiously, I place a hand on Vel's chest and swing a leg over. As my body touches his, a sudden jolt hits me, my breath hitching as I press against him, confused by the physical effect he's having on me. I'm a heartbeat away from burying my face into his neck and staying where I am. This dragon smells like the enticing spiced scents sold at the markets, exotic and expensive. Yet this is more, as if I can *taste* that smell.

This insanity happened with Cam too—I'll need to keep physical contact with these creatures to a minimum. I slide myself across Vel's wide torso, my thighs moving across his muscular ones. Even though he's not aroused in the slightest, the heat from Vel's body warms more than my blood.

I pause. What the fuck is wrong with me?

An arm bands my waist, and I take a sudden breath as a hand slides into my hair and yanks my head back. Eyes with blood red irises look into mine, pupils dark.

"What are you doing?" he asks gruffly.

Even with my head back, our faces are close, and I squirm as his arm holds me harder to him. "Uh. I need to relieve myself."

His mouth curves into the first smile I've seen. "I hope you mean you need to visit the bathroom to achieve this relief, and not by rubbing yourself against me."

I choke in shock. "No! Please let me go."

Velanor's fingers remain threaded in my hair, his mouth now parted as he looks up at me. "You could've asked me to move instead of climbing around on top of me."

"You were asleep."

"Unconscious. When did you attempt to poison me?"

"I didn't!"

64

Velanor lifts his head, face closer. "Then why did I feel disoriented for a short while?"

Not long enough. My chest tightens—I'm lying on top of the dragon who threatened to hurt me and who I definitely injured.

And other reasons. I attempt to move my hips away from him, and he sucks air between his teeth. "I agreed not to touch you, yet you've decided to seductively writhe around on me."

"Excuse me?" I retort, face hotter still. "I am not—"

Velanor interrupts with a raucous laugh and releases my hair. Again, I attempt to move but his arm bands like steel around my waist.

"I'd like to move now, Velanor," I say, pushing against his chest so our mouths stay far, far apart.

"How are you doing that?" he asks, voice gravelly.

"Doing what?"

"I'm sure you're aware *what*." He moves again for emphasis and triggers an unwanted ache in my core as his hardened cock pushes between us. *No.* "Using your Ebon seduction? Pointless. I don't fuck those I hate."

"Shut up!" I snap. "I don't want to fuck you."

"I can smell that you do." He smirks when my eyes widen. "Cam obviously *wasn't* enough."

"Only because you're a dragon and have this effect on my body. My mind is not in agreement. At all."

Velanor's fingers curl around my face and his lips almost touch mine. "Yes. I would not put my cock inside something Ebon. Don't waste your time."

"You're disgusting," I retort and succeed in rolling off him, landing inelegantly on the floor in the small space between the bed and door. "I only climbed on you to try to get away."

Velanor doesn't respond with the smart comment I

expected and when I look up his eyes are closed and mouth open, face softened by sleep. Or unconsciousness.

My racing heart speeds with urgency as I carefully slide a hand into his boot. Locating my dagger, I tuck the blade into my own boot then turn to the door.

CHAPTER 10

AURELIA

I'M SHAKING AS I SLOWLY LOWER THE DOOR HANDLE, fearful Velanor might wake again but he doesn't move. Will he know what I did once he awakes?

And what do I do now? Four dragons are toying with me, fighting to win a game. Therefore, one will find me. Which dragon would I *want* to? I've no idea how the Emerald and Ivory princes might treat me, but of *these* two, Cam is my preference. If I manage to hide from Velanor tonight and he hasn't flown from the ship looking for me, I'll wait at the docks and look for Cam.

The thought causes my teeth to grind. What I *really* want to do is return to Westport or the Aureate court.

The inn has quietened since I retired, partly due to those asleep on tables, others in their rooms, I suppose. Seb wipes down the bar, a pointless task because the place will be filthy again within hours and his rag doesn't look the cleanest.

He glances up. "Problem with the dragon? I couldn't fathom why he was with you."

"I've decided to find somewhere better to sleep." His lips thin. "More room, I mean. I appreciate your hospitality, Seb."

Seb grunts. "And if the dragon looks for you?"

"Tell him I left. Simple."

"Hmm." A chair scrapes behind me and I turn in alarm, as a man slides to the floor. "Sailors are good for business, but they make a hell of a lot of work," Seb grumbles as he glares at him.

"If you see Devin, tell him I'd like him and Luin to visit Reodian," I say quietly.

"Why?"

What do I tell Seb? I chew my lip. "I'm visiting the dragons and would like him to join me."

"Dragons don't allow humans and elves into their courts."

"I'm *lucky*." Or not. I flash him a smile. "I won't tell you where I'm going once I leave the inn, but the dragon might be... insistent. So, tell him I headed to the King's Arms."

He shakes his head and sighs. "Ria. Don't mess with dragons."

"I'm not. They're messing with me." With every word, my gaze darts between Seb and the door leading to the stairs in case a furious dragon appears. "I need to go."

As I move around bodies and tables to the door, I grab a cloak from the floor that somebody discarded or lost and swing the ale-soaked item around my shoulders. At least the wool is thick and the cloak long.

The cool night air hits my cheeks and I yank up the hood, looking from side to side. There's little difference between here and Westport, a mixture of classes and races from different realms; an easy place to lose yourself in. Another of Devin's friends lives at the opposite edge of town, a short walk past the docks, and Ned never asks questions.

Head up, imitating a male gait, I stride away, dagger hilt now pressed against my palm. Again, I wait for an angry dragon to seize me, but only humans and elves walk the streets, some staggering, others shouting out to each other. I scrutinize anybody who lurks beneath darkened eaves, especially if they're alone. One man watches closely as I pass by and after a swift sizing up of him, I'm no longer worried. His portly figure could pin me down, but he'd never get a chance to touch me before I retaliated.

The path splits, downwards to the docked boats and upwards towards where the buildings become crowded. I pass a group of men sitting on the low stone wall above the sloping pathway towards the boats. They're playing dice beneath the dim street lanterns as they swig from bottles. Sailors removed from the taverns?

I reach the central marketplace where empty wooden stalls run in rows through the cobbled plaza, close to where the pathway leads either upwards or down to the docks. I love searching through the curiosities some bring to the markets but there's no chance that I'll browse tomorrow. I'll be long gone, hopefully.

Another man moves through the shrouded town, heading along the street in my direction. I straighten my shoulders and prepare to stride onwards; I'm a woman alone, but I know these streets.

As the man moves closer, I'm a heartbeat from turning and running instead because he's taller than he looked at a distance.

Inhumanly muscular.

"You have to be fucking kidding me," I mutter as the man veers towards me.

Dragon.

He stands uncomfortably close, but in the dim, I can't

69

make out the color of his hair. "For fuck's sake. Another. Which one are you?"

His laugh is low and gruff. "Another? I presume you mean which dragon prince? Emerald flight."

"What's your name, Emerald Prince?" I snap.

"Lucanor."

Fortunately, there's no room for him to shift without breaking the stalls apart, so I hold my ground. "And are you as big an asshole as your friends?"

Lucanor pulls my hood back, and my mouth dries. His intense eyes are bright enough to see the unnatural green as he touches my cheek with rough fingertips. "That depends on how you behave, Aurelia."

I step back as again the weird buzz happens with him too. "Velanor will be pissed if you take me."

"Ha! I knew the bastard was on to you. Him and Cam suddenly became very interested in the port towns." He scratches his neck. "Didn't Cam find you?"

"Yes." I clench my teeth. "We were sailing and then Velanor dragged me from the ship and flew with me in his paws."

For a moment, Lucanor gawks at me before laughing again. "Cam will be pissed. Where *is* Vel?" He lifts his head and sniffs. "I can smell him on you, but he isn't here. Running from him?"

"I was walking."

Lucanor's chest rumbles in amusement again. "I'm surprised he didn't take you to Reodian. You *do* know that's where Vel and Cam planned to take you?"

"Yep."

"Then where is he?"

"Sleeping."

Footsteps thump on the cobbled street behind and Lucanor falls silent. Hairs on my arms lift. *Please don't hurt me.*

"Where did you come from?" snaps Lucanor.

Fuck. I whirl around, almost nose to chest, with the dragon behind.

Not Velanor. Thank the gods.

"When three of you home in on one place, there's a reason." His sonorous voice has a lilt to match the others, and my powers of deduction tell me he's the Ivory exarch. He smiles, but these dragons' smiles are never friendly. Not totally.

"And you are?" I ask with a sigh.

"I'm Elianor of the Ivory flight." He flourishes a hand and bows. "I'm happy to meet you, Aurelia. You look every bit as lovely as I thought."

I scoff. "In the dark?" His lips purse, and he exchanges a wry smile with Lucanor. "And you both have a problem."

"Yes?" Elianor arches a brow. "I believe you're the one with the problem."

"I *believe* you plan to take me to Reodian in one piece, not two halves. And I know you're all playing a game and that whoever takes me to your elders first wins." I swallow down the sourness in my mouth. "Which is disgusting behavior, by the way."

"Nobody in the human and elven realms would tell us where you were, Aurelia," says Lucanor. "We had no choice but to hunt you."

Hunt. I shuffle so I'm no longer half-trapped between them. "Now I am beginning to realize why nobody would tell you."

"She's right about the problem, Luc," puts in Elianor. "Only one of us can win."

"How about you fight over me, and I'll sit over there?" I point to a wall. "I can wait until you decide who wins."

I've barely taken one step before biting fingers surround

my upper arm. "And run while we're distracted?" says Elianor wryly. "You're smarter than that."

"She has a point, Eli," says Luc and turns his gleaming eyes to mine. "Two of us—and we weren't the first to find her. Would it even be fair for one of us to take Aurelia?"

Eli snorts. "Sounds like Vel is already playing unfair."

"Then what?" he replies.

The grip on my upper arm remains. "Take her to the island," says Eli. "The others will head back when they need to rest."

"Island?" I choke out. "What island?"

"The dragon isle in the Western Seas. Has your mother never told you the story about the place?" asks Eli. I blink at him. "The place the Sapphire guardian took her and where she claimed the First-Born eggs?"

Lucanor grunts. "As Cam likes to frequently remind us. Sapphire are *so* much cleverer than the other flights because Luin helped with the rebirth."

Oh, fuck. *That* island. Nobody passes on ships since there's no merchant route through that part of the seas, and the island is far out from the closest shore.

Alone with four dragons. Cut off from the world. Suddenly, a city full of them becomes appealing. "Or Reodian? Take me there."

"We can't unless we agree who won," explains Luc.

"Won." I spit the word. "You're disgusting and immoral to treat a person like this."

Eli leans down and runs his tongue along his too-sharp teeth. "Perhaps thank the stars we are noble dragons and less *disgusting* than the *immoral* dragons who normally frequent the human inns."

"Noble? Like Velanor? He threatened to break my arm," I snap back. "And I stabbed him, and I will do so again if I'm threatened."

Eli gawks at me. "*Stabbed* him?"

"Disarm her," says Luc brusquely.

Before I catch up to what's happening, Eli has one arm around my neck and the other around my waist while Luc's hands pat along my hips. Fingers probe around my upper thigh, searching for a sheath, moving way too far upwards.

"Do you mind?" I struggle against Eli, and I'm a heartbeat from kicking Luc in the face for his groping. "My weapon is in my boot, not attached to my leg." Instead, I take a calming breath as Luc extracts the dagger.

His eyes narrow as he holds the blade and looks at the hilt. "Ebon dagger."

My stomach lurches at his hate-laced voice. "Ebon elves aren't your enemy any longer."

Luc's lips pull back in an animalistic snarl. "We'll never trust anything Ebon."

"Including you." Eli's warm breath tickles my ear and I struggle against him again, digging short nails into his bare arm. "And keep still, unless you're intending to arouse me."

I abruptly stop, muttering expletives under my breath. I'm pissed that I'm in this position when normally I can either pre-empt an attack or find my way out of an opponent's grip. I don't believe anything could escape a dragon's hold and I don't want to provoke him further in any way.

"Let me go. We've established I won't run and now you have my weapon." Eli's arms release me, and I stumble forward as Luc continues to study the dagger, carefully running a finger along the edge.

And those aren't nails at the tips. I swallow.

"Stabbed Vel?" His brow raises higher. "The man isn't known for his calm nature. You were lucky."

"I wouldn't say luck smiled upon me in recent days. And I don't want to go to your island," I say and cross my arms.

"Did anybody *ask* if you wanted to?" asks Eli and they both chuckle at me. "Don't worry, dragons don't sleep in caves. We've a comfortable place to stay and that stay won't be long."

"Oh, how marvelous. An island holiday," I say sarcastically. "Do your princely servants live there too?"

"Gods, she'll be a pain in the ass, I can tell," says Eli.

Yes. I intend to be.

"Should we find Vel before we leave?" asks Luc.

"Fuck. No." I straighten. "He'll be pissed with me."

Elianor lifts his head and appears to sniff again. "Yes. Why isn't he following? How hard did you stab him?"

"Um. Not hard." I blow air into my cheeks. "He's sleeping, so I snuck away."

Their faces are plastered with suspicion. "Then you should leave with us before he wakes," says Elianor. "Since Luc wants to be *noble* about this and wait for Vel and Cam on the island."

They have a point, but *island*.

"Fly?" I croak out.

"We're not walking. That's two days at a human pace. You've flown on a dragon's back before. Luinor is one of your mother's consorts."

Consorts. I chuckle at the word. "Yes. I know your magic will hold me to your back. Flying doesn't bother me; what happens to me on that island does."

Luc crosses his arms. "Nobody will harm you. I give you my word."

The word of a dragon hunting me? "Even Vel?"

The two glance at each other. "He has been warned. You've inflamed the situation, but we'll rein him in."

The dragon with a temper who I stabbed then escaped from. Hmm. Can they?

Earlier tonight, I traveled with a dragon prince towards his once fabled city, but I never imagined a second would abduct me from the ship, *or* that a third and fourth prince would take me to a deserted island.

Again, I am *not* having a good night.

CHAPTER 11

AURELIA

THESE DRAGONS ARE TERRIFYING, LEAST OF ALL BECAUSE they're bigger than Luin, both in length and bulk with wings twice as wide as their bodies. When Velanor swooped on the ship, he was almost half the length of the vessel, and these are no different. The dragons' scales shimmer brighter even in poor light and a single paw could stomp a man to death in one hit—or a misbehaving woman they're abducting. I've always struggled with matching dragon to man in my mind, puzzled by how any creature can shift between two forms, and always saw Luin and his dragon as separate entities.

There's some discussion who I fly with before we walk to a place large enough for them to shift and with less spectators, including me. I have no say in the matter and in the end, Eli takes me on his back.

The wind rushes past my face, eyes stinging, and I'm grateful that he only flies straight once he ascends above the world. I've flown high before, but never as far. As the dragon follows the coastline, we reach stretches of high cliffs that the lead-colored seas batter and spray against. I grip onto his wide shoulders and the magic pins me to him as if a large weight rests on me, pushing my chest down, lungs aching. Pressed against Eli's soft, scaled back, arms around his neck, I clench my jaw as I remember the inelegant and unpleasant way Velanor carried me and how he could've dropped me.

And then the inelegant way I sprawled across him in that bed.

Is he conscious yet?

I've no fear that I'll fall as I can't move my body and barely my head. The first time I flew on Luin, I vomited once I climbed from his back, as the spell had pressed my guts so hard against him that I felt as if every organ would escape. Therefore, I'm accustomed to the queasiness and thankfully won't embarrass myself by retching up my guts in front of these dragons.

The small island looks as if it's merely a lump of rock that one day jutted from the ocean and stayed above. Surely something pure stone would be uninhabitable. The place is close enough to the mainland to allow a boat to easily cross but too far for all but the strongest swimmer to reach. I can't swim so there's no chance I'd even attempt to anyway.

Eli lands on a pebbled shore and releases me. My attempt to casually climb down from him fails as I slip and land on my backside on the damp ground. The reverberating noise he makes teaches me how dragons laugh in their shifted forms, and I growl back at him as I stand and brush myself off. Luc hovers above and Eli joins him, the pair gliding towards the island's center.

They're shifting out of sight again. Do the pair think I'll faint from shock? Watching and hearing bones crack and sinew tear isn't pleasant and admittedly did scare me when I peeked at Luin shifting once, but I find the whole process shockingly fascinating. How vulnerable are dragons in their halfway state?

In an attempt to forget what's happening, I dodge the lapping water, amusing myself by jumping back and forth as the seas reach my booted toes. One path leads upwards from the cove I'm in, through the craggy gray rock that rises several meters above the shore. I hope this 'comfortable' place to sleep exists.

The pair return, back in their male forms. Silhouetted in the night, their size and determined gait unnerves me as much as their dragons.

Luc pauses in front of me. "Let's go."

"Far? I've been awake half the night and I'm bloody tired."

Eli chuckles. "A short walk, even for little human legs. And you may rest. We can't do anything until the others arrive."

Oh, they could do plenty. But I stay quiet.

My aching legs pull me along the path, and the dragons kick up pebbles as they walk. We reach a surprisingly flattened area where a wide pool shimmers bright blue despite the night sky. Closer in size to a small lake, I can see to the other side, but walking around would take a minute. The moon strokes the pool in rippling beams, but the water remains still. The island's rock surrounds us like a tall wall hiding the interior from anybody who might pass on the seas.

Boulders offer places to sit around the pool and a grass-like plant springs underfoot as we move towards the trees surrounding the water. I don't know the whole story about my family's visit to the island all those years ago, but picture them sitting around the pool. Were they all close then? They're a mismatched group—the human and elven high lords, a Lightbringer knight, an assassin, and a dragon.

Calla once whispered a story that Luin never wanted me

to know; a secret about the life the pair spent together long before the five met.

I'm not sure I believe her.

The thin line of trees opens into a clearing with a narrow two-story home that looks as if it's been lifted from an elven court and dropped into the middle of the trees. The building is squashed into the space where trees once stood, which almost reach the doors and windows.

Despite the wild location, the building eclipses those in splendorous elven courts. But unlike the elven houses, this one doesn't blend into the woods, instead appearing like a jewel inset into the trees. Do buildings in Reodian have the same high-domed roofs glowing in the moonlight?

A long verandah spans the front with stone benches facing towards us. As we approach, I can see details that dragons own this place, the flights' colors painted around the doorframe. The shining silver doors are the point any resemblance to the surroundings ends as I step into a room as richly furnished as any court I've attended. The opulence within shouldn't surprise me either, considering the dragons possess troves filled with valuable and beautiful items they collect. Everything in their world is bright, and the dragons' choice of silver-colored floor tiles and white-painted walls continues that brilliance.

The room is crammed with expense—not only the gilded furniture but shelves holding jeweled figurines and other statues of dragons around. I also see the two dragons clearly for the first time as the lanterns are lit, and they're every bit as striking as Cam and Velanor. I've encountered every color dragon over the last few years, but the exarchs' hue is turned up a notch. Luc's emerald hair shimmers as the lantern gives it tones that are almost silver, his eyes a brighter green than I thought possible.

Eli's features are similar to the other dragons', but his

watery blue eyes give him a closer appearance to a human. In the flickering light, he's a ghostly version of his friend, skin even paler than a Lumen elf's.

I stand on the shining marble floor and look around. "You have no fire."

Luc bursts into laughter. "That is the first thing you notice?"

I scowl. "How do you cook? Stay warm?"

"Outside, if we do, and dragons don't get cold." Eli passes me. "Are *you* cold?"

"A little." I gesture at myself. "These clothes are all I have and I chose them for spending time in a ship's cabin warmed by fire."

The pair glance at each other. "We don't have many blankets. Perhaps we could keep you warm?" suggests Eli.

I huff at the obviousness of his statement and stride over, tipping my head back in order to meet his eyes. His full, sensuous lips are pursed, those eyes sparkling, and I'm fascinated by how smooth his skin appears.

"If you've brought me here in the belief I'll fall at your feet and lie with you because you're irresistible, think again." That mouth tips into a smile and creates a dimple in one cheek. *A dragon with a dimple.*

Eli's eyes drop to my lips and drift lower, appraising what he can see, as I'm also clearer to view. "What if I fell at yours, Aurelia?" he says, the seductive tone sending a shiver from scalp to toes. His face moves closer, the dragon essence behind his cedar scent drifting towards me. "What if I were to do everything you instructed?"

I swallow hard. A dragon kneeling at my feet? He's teasing, but I'm aroused at the thought of any man doing such. And by his light laugh, Eli knows.

"Everything?" I reply, copying his tone. He moistens his lips and nods. "Then I'd like wine. That will warm me up."

Luc shoves Eli. "What are you whispering about?"

"Aurelia is making demands of me." His darkened gaze remains on my lips. "Perhaps she thinks she's a princess due to her Ebon essence."

"She's practically an elven princess, remember?" Luc nods at me. "Or whatever the Lumen High Lords call their offspring."

I balk as he runs his nose along my cheek, the touch barely there but adding to the aching arousal. What the fuck is with my reaction to these creatures? "But she has the essence, too."

"Keep your nose off me," I retort and step back, more annoyed when he laughs again.

"As you wish. Just let me know should you want any other of my body parts touching you."

"Elianor." Luc pushes him. "Can you not? Do you want Aurelia to run screaming from the house?"

"No. But the screaming part sounds interesting."

"Wine?" I say, ignoring Eli's attempt to fluster me.

"Yes, Princess." With one last smirk, he wanders away through an archway.

"Is this what all dragons are like?" I ask. "I would've thought *royal* ones less... base than the ones who frequent our towns."

His fascinating eyes glint. "Dragons are physical creatures in all respects. What would your race call us? Primal." He flashes his sharp canines in a smile. "And if you've lived with one, then you'll know we're plain speaking."

"Blunt, rude, and arrogant?" I ask.

"Well, *you* have the blunt and rude part of your dragon essence," he comments. "Perhaps primal in your choice of... profession. I'd wager that your physical appetites are influenced by this essence, too."

"For fuck's sake! Are dragons all obsessed with sex?" I

shake my head as I prove his point. "You'd better all hope that I've nothing *else* from this Ebon essence that might erupt if you try to touch me."

His expression switches so quickly from friendly amusement to dark disgust that I involuntarily back away. Luc's pupils become slits within the vibrant green and his lips pull back, baring sharper teeth than moments ago.

"I hope," he says in a harsh voice, "that this is not a threat from a girl who's discovered and embraced the Ebon Queen's power."

The room grows colder, my blood slushing at how the friendliest of the four has shifted mood so quickly. "No." I clear my throat. "That was an idle threat. I've never, *ever* sensed the Ebon."

But the dreams. The ones I never speak about—noises in the dark that become shapes and voices, as I look through the eyes of another. Recently, the forms became clearer, elven, committing horrors before me.

And the night that Devin refuses to speak to me about.

"What's behind your eyes, Aurelia?" Luc's harshness continues.

"Nothing."

"And you said that *I'd* send her screaming from the house?" A mug is shoved into my hand, Eli's fingers brushing mine, and I jerk at the shock between our skin. He doesn't react. "What's with the teeth and eyes display, Luc?"

I gulp wine and almost choke at the strength. This isn't wine, and the sweetness doesn't disguise the potency.

Luc blinks away the dragon. "Reminding Aurelia who has the power here." My heart continues to race at his undertone, but my shoulders relax when he doesn't mention my failed half-joke.

"And you're the nicest, too." Eli pinches Luc's cheek. "If

this situation comes down to powers of persuasion, you're not off to a good start."

"What does that mean?" I ask.

Eli slurps from his own cup. "If we can't choose who's won, you might need to decide."

The room sways slightly as exhaustion catches up. I choose? Unlikely. A few hours ago, I ate supper with a ship's captain and considered the soft bed waiting in his cabin. Since then, all manner of unexpected and unwanted things have happened to me. How long until dawn? I yawn, regretting the wine.

"You look like shit, Aurelia," comments Eli.

"How charming," I retort.

"Tired, I mean." He jerks his chin indicating above us. "Sleep. We'll talk tomorrow."

"Sleep where?" I ask suspiciously.

"You can have Cam's bed. I doubt he'll return before tomorrow."

"Are you sure?" I narrow my eyes.

"And we won't touch you or take you anywhere. We've more honor than Vel and think returning with you is unfair to Cam."

Luc's continued silence after our exchange warns me that I might be unsafe, but I'm too tired to deal with anything else. I stifle another yawn. "You owe me an explanation on why you're doing this. Who you are. What will happen to me? Cam lied, and Vel hardly told me anything."

"And then will you cooperate?" asks Eli and crosses his arms.

I eye how the muscles bulge. "If you promise to respect me as a person and not a thing in a game."

His face splits into a huge grin. "Oh, you're absolutely *not* a thing. I, for one, am very keen to get to know you."

"That!" I jab a finger at him, and his eyes widen. "That comment worries me—you might climb into my bed."

"You're extremely suspicious of us," he replies.

Are they *serious*? "Apart from the whole abduction and cat-and-mouse game, dragons are known for their less than controlled physical side."

"True," says Luc quietly, hardness still in his tone. "Aurelia, you have our word that nothing will happen to you either in or out of the bed you sleep in."

"Such as choosing whether to go home or not?" I ask hopefully and pointlessly.

The pair look at each other. "You know that isn't possible."

CHAPTER 12

AURELIA

I WAKE TO MORNING SUN THAT HURTS MY EYES AND IS intensified by the light hitting the gold chandelier and lanterns almost blinding me. The room's perfection is marred by the stack of unfamiliar clothes thrown over the chair and scuffed, dirty boots beside them. I leap out of bed, on guard in case Cam's naked nearby. After their behavior a few hours ago, I'd half-expected to find a dragon in the room, perhaps standing in the floor to ceiling window or sitting in the low chair beside the door to a small bathing room. Nobody, thank the gods.

The large bed I slept in seems small for a dragon although certainly larger than the one I'd begun the night in with Velanor.

Velanor. I moisten my dry lips.

Has he arrived and waits downstairs this morning? If Cam or Velanor returned last night, they did so quietly which I can't imagine happening, particularly as Eli and Luc spent a long time talking to each other loudly. I'd hoped to overhear something helpful but most of their conservation was about evenings drinking and the women they spent time with and exactly *how* they spent that time. Disgusted with their crudeness, I'd placed a cushion over my head and curled up beneath the blanket Eli found me before he showed me to the room.

Not without more suggestive comments, which I was too exhausted to respond to.

Dressing quickly, I stand by the bedroom doorway, ear pressed to the wood and listen for voices. Silence. I sneak from the room and down the open, slatted wooden stairs. Yawning, I take a quick look around the sitting room take a large red apple from a bowl in the center of a round table and pour water from a jug.

I drink and eat quickly and I'm out of the house as fast as possible, heading towards the pool before a dragon appears.

And now? What happens? Because this competition to find me first has failed and they need some way to decide who returns to the First-Born with me, triumphant. I don't like that Eli hinted the dragons might toy with me between themselves. If so, they can forget any cooperation.

Stars, what will happen to me? Thirty days is a long time.

The pool in the island's center shines an impossible azure blue, more vibrant than the brightest summer skies, even though the day is hazy with cloud. I perch on one of the larger boulders, the white surface hard to get purchase on, although close enough to dip my toes.

Before I chose to place my feet into the water, I paused, unsure what magic a dragon pool might contain, but when I saw the shimmering silver scales from a fish below, I decided this water must sustain life not disintegrate any body part dipped inside. Besides, my mother once swam in this pool.

The water's warmth surprises me; any lake or pool I've

encountered has felt cooler than the surroundings, but this one matches fresh bath water. My reflection blurs with the ripples, my tired eyes and untied hair disappearing.

"Aurelia."

How can a dragon sneak? Because Luc succeeded. I tense as he approaches with something in his hand, the sun picking out viridian within his emerald hair. I can't help appraising his impressive body, eyes again drawn to the forearms. These men have a beauty in their human form at odds with the monstrous dragons, too damn attractive for something that spends time as a deadly creature.

"Ria," I reply. "I'd appreciate if you used that name."

He smiles, showing less teeth than last night. "Of course."

I eye him warily as he moves closer still. "I can't run away. I'll come back to the house soon," I say.

As he stands over me, my gaze goes to where he's holding a bunched up, bulging piece of green cloth in one hand and—impressively—holding two goblets by the stems and a bottle containing a yellow liquid in his other. He places this on the boulder beside me and unwraps the cloth, revealing dried meat and a flat bread, then hands me a goblet.

"We don't have a lot to eat here," he says apologetically.

"I ate an apple."

His mouth curves into a smile and I shake my head at the absurdity of the situation as he pours from the bottle into my goblet. "I wanted to apologize for my behavior last night. I was tired and frustrated with the situation." His voice and manner couldn't be more opposite to his harsh treatment. He didn't say another word to me before Eli showed me to Cam's room.

I sip the liquid, tart yet sweet—apple juice. "Is that what you all think?" I ask. "You practically accused me of being the Ebon Queen herself. Until Cam found me, I'd no awareness who I am."

"May I?" Luc gestures at the space beside me on the boulder and I shrug. He sits to my left and his hip touches mine, powerful thigh against my leg.

Stupid heart racing, I look at the water instead of him. "Is Eli awake? Can we talk now?"

"No, still sleeping." He nods at the food. "Eat. I don't often prepare breakfast for people."

"Is such an act beneath your station as a dragon prince?" I ask and arch a brow.

"Something like that. Be grateful this meal isn't something I attempted to cook." He watches as I tear a piece of the meat between my teeth and struggle to chew. I've eaten beef jerky before and always found the saltiness and texture disagreeable, but I smile politely before switching to the heavy bread. "The others haven't returned yet," he adds.

"I guessed that. I'm sure I would've heard Vel if *he* had." I grimace.

Luc rests back, palms on the stone behind him as he tips his face to the sky. "Oh, yes. Vel will be 'fun' to deal with. But don't worry about him."

A cold shiver runs through me at their warning about his temper. If only I could believe that I don't need to worry. "What will happen next?"

"I'm unsure. Once Cam and Vel return, we can discuss what to do between ourselves."

I snort. "Of course, and the poor little human does as the dragons decide."

When he doesn't reply, I turn my head to him. Keen eyes meet mine. "No. I believe you should be involved in the decision."

Choking out a laugh, I wriggle my toes in the water. "A decision about *what* though? Tell me everything about this little challenge of yours."

He leans over me to take the jerky from the cloth to my

right and effortlessly slices through with his teeth, chewing contemplatively as I wait. "We mean you no harm, Ria. We're following orders from our First-Born."

"A little competition for their princes?" I ask coolly. "Proving your worth?"

He shakes his head. "We work with and for our elders. They aid us in learning our positions at the head of our courts."

I have to admit to myself that I'm intrigued by how their society works. The dragons guard their realm against the outside world, and few enter. Those who do get no further than the central city, Reodian, where the First-Born elders reside. Even that place is hard to reach as the city is suspended high above the world. One way to avoid an invasion, I guess.

Nobody seems to know what dragon courts are like—even how big they are—only that there's one for each flight headed by chosen exarchs. The princes. I'd expected them to be elder dragons too, but they can't be much older than me.

Strangely, my invitation could be seen as an honor.

Oh wait, not invited. *Taken.*

"You could've *asked* me," I say. "Why pursue me around the lands?"

"Hmm." He drinks his juice. "I believe the elders wanted us to show our power, just in case—"

"In case I exploded into Ebon evil?" I sound sarcastic but, I'm scared.

"Yes." I straighten. Fuck. "Ria, even though the Ebon flight was eradicated, the First-Born became aware that Ebon essence still existed somewhere outside the dragon realms, and naturally suspicion landed on your family. The elders knew that should they approach, your parents would take any child deeper into hiding. We need to know if the essence they felt is from you or elsewhere. And so, the elders issued a challenge to the four of us—find Calla's daughter."

"Out of duty? Vel hinted there's a 'prize'."

Luc purses his lips, looking over the water again. In the silence, something strikes me. There's no birdsong in the trees surrounding us, only an occasional seabird flying high overhead, silent.

"In return, the elders are offering a closer relationship with them—extra power to the one who achieved this."

"What power?" I ask sharply.

"Currently, we hold lower positions and spend time training to become what the First-Born wish their exarchs to be. The courts are still being rebuilt and until we meet their standards, they won't trust us to oversee our flight. I suspect they're also looking for one of us to take a key role within Reodian. Although the First-Born spend most of their time in the city, Talindra—the Ruby First-Born, our queen—dislikes the place and presumably wants to hand some control of the city to another."

"One of you," I say. "But why do they need to see me?"

I expect Luc to avert his eyes, try to hide that he's lying, but he looks clearly back at me. "To deduce how much essence you contain and whether you're dangerous."

I stiffen. "They do want to hurt me!"

"No. They might persuade you to stay but won't harm you."

"Uh." I stand, balancing on the rock. "'Persuade'. Such as imprisoning me?"

"Not at all."

I laugh at him. "How else do you 'persuade' someone to stay who doesn't want to?"

"Everybody has their price." He leans forward to run long fingers through the water, emerald hair falling into his eyes. "Especially mercenaries."

"I don't want to go to Reodian," I blurt. "Take me somewhere else. Tell the elders that you couldn't find me."

He tilts his head. "Ria, you know that's impossible."

"If I don't return after thirty days, people from my father's court will look for me. Luin will come."

"I trust the First-Born to do the right thing by you and your people. The dragons don't want more conflict. We'd rather be left alone." He shakes the water from his hand. "None of the princes want instability either. Hence, we won't allow anything untoward to happen."

Even the Ruby one? I bite my lip. "I've heard enough tales about the First-Born to know they don't negotiate."

"They allowed your mother to live," he says simply.

"Because Luin took her as a mate." My breath catches. "Is *that* what they're planning?" I stumble from the rock. "Oh, no. Fuck, no. I'm not bonding with any of you."

His laugh bounces on the water. "The bonds are an archaic means of control. We no longer take a 'mate', otherwise how would us princes have the fun we do?"

I relax—slightly.

"Besides, we need heirs. Why would the First-Born bond a dragon prince with a human who can't bear dragon children?"

"Lay eggs?" I ask.

This time the mirth comes louder, and he stands too. "We don't lay eggs. Some dragons' souls were kept in gems and because humans like to focus on the fantastical, they called them eggs. These clutches of gems were hidden by each flight during the war and could only be 'hatched' by the First-Born. Once the flights' First-Born returned, they used their essence on the eggs, these souls were made corporeal, and the courts were recreated. The *new* dragons birthed offspring and so our realms are repopulating."

"Dragons have children like humans?" I ask.

91

"Well, dragons fuck like humans." He chuckles. "Mostly."

"Funny." Damp fingers touch my cheek and I search his face for any inclination he's telling me stories. "Is this all the truth, Luc?"

His other hand touches my cheek too, both now held between his large fingers, warm. Firm. "I promise that nobody will harm you, and my word is my honor. Always."

Tears prick my eyes as the events of the last few days catch up. Until now, the surreal feeling I have from events has distanced me from reality. I could cope but each horrible thing that happens hammers home that this *is* real. "I hope you keep that promise. And that 'nobody' includes you."

"Ria." I startle when he places his lips on my forehead and holds them for a few seconds. "Emerald flight are healers not fighters." He withdraws. "Diplomats."

I don't tell him that I can't imagine a dragon practicing diplomacy and force a smile as I push back the tears. I won't allow Luc to see them.

"Come with me. We'll speak with Eli and explain more. As I promised." He gestures towards the tall trees the house lurks in the middle of.

Two shapes as high as the clouds streaking the sky catch my eye and I squint in the bright sunshine. My stomach lurches once the figures become clearer.

Two dragons, and I can guess who.

Luc shades his face as he watches them. As the pair move lower, the sunlight glints on scales and a sapphire dragon dives straight at a ruby one—Vel, whose wings then push outwards, knocking Cam away and preventing his rival touching him.

Swearing under his breath, Luc hops off the boulder. I'm transfixed by the swooping and climbing, at their rearing up in the sky against each other. By the time the dragons reach the tree line, Cam lurches straight at Vel and their bodies collide. Branches crack as the pair plunge into the canopies.

"Are they... fighting?" I ask and turn to Luc. He's no longer beside me, now halfway around the edge of the pool, running at an inhuman speed in the direction of their descent.

"Wait there," he calls back.

Luc knows nothing about me if he thinks I'll follow barked orders.

CHAPTER 13

AURELIA

As Luc hurtles into the trees, the opposite direction to the house, I set off after him, pebbles digging into my bare feet. Smaller sticks on the ground poke at my soles as I reach the dense wooded area and cautiously move forward.

The trunks and branches are further apart than the last woods I ran through, and daylight helps, even though I wish I'd shoved my boots on first. I hear the dragons before I see them, their snarling and shouting echoing through the broken woods, the pair now two men who're struggling with each other between the torn trunks.

As I step closer, I almost back off. Yes, the Ruby and Sapphire princes are in male form, but not quite. The longer nails are talon size, scales covering half their faces like scars, and I'm not moving any further forward because even from this vantage point I can see sharper teeth.

Amongst the destruction, Luc shouts at them to stop, sharing my common sense not to get between the vicious pair. Heavy boots sound on the ground behind and I yelp as Eli catches my arm.

At the sound, Vel's head snaps around, glowing eyes focusing on me. In a heartbeat, he's torn me from Eli's hands and my body floods with terror as I'm slammed against the nearest trunk, a hand around my throat, talons scraping the side of my neck. His scratched face streaks with blood and I swear there's some on his teeth too.

"What did you do to me?" His voice is deeper, edged by an animalistic snarl. When I don't reply, he grips harder, blood-red irises glowing. "Tell me what you did you fucking —" In a reflex move, my knee collides with his crotch, admittedly harder than I'd usually hit and he roars at me.

The chokehold doesn't loosen until Luc wrenches his arm away, Eli pulling the other until Vel's trapped, arms behind his back, but struggling to lash out at them. His growling breaths and feral focus on me don't ease.

I don't experience this often but I'm absolutely fucking terrified. My legs tremble and I hold my neck where he half-choked me, rooted to the ground by shock.

Cam steps around the three, and only his odd eyes remain from his dragon form as he outstretches a hand. "Come with me."

I continue to tremble as I stare at his broad palm.

No. I press my back against the trunk, hair caught on the bark as I shake my head. Cam snarls but not at me, before spinning and landing a fist in Vel's face.

This time the crack isn't from branches and Vel's shouting grows louder.

"What the fuck are you doing, Vel? You don't hurt a woman." Blood drips from Vel's broken nose, and Cam's face almost touches his as they stand chest to chest.

"You think that's what she is?" He looks past Luc at me

with a fury that stops my heart. "Would a woman stab a dragon and then fucking poison him?"

"I didn't poison you," I rasp out.

He no longer struggles against his friends, but the cold anger doesn't leave his face.

"Take Ria back to the house, Cam." says Luc softly. "We'll deal with the asshole."

Cam reaches out to me, but I jerk away from him before he can make contact. Again, running is useless, but I move away from them into the woods at a faster pace.

"Ria. Wait. You know I won't hurt you," he calls and falls into step alongside me, not touching.

"Take me to Reodian," I say. "Get me away from *him*." I stride onwards until I reach the house. "Otherwise, I'll take my chances and swim."

Cam takes my arm again. "Vel won't hurt you."

"*Really*? So that was a friendly hello?" I retort.

"He's pissed for a few reasons, including that he was losing the fight against me. Vel will calm down." But his smile doesn't fool me.

"Is this what happens when any of you get angry?" I swallow down the lump rising in my throat. "I'm not safe."

"Vel isn't coming into the house until he's less feral. You're safe."

Feral. "That doesn't answer my question."

Cam touches my cheek. "As you charmingly told me, I'm rude and arrogant but I'm not quick-tempered. Ruby flight dragons are aggressive. You chose the wrong one to assault." His warm palm triggers that strange connection from when he kissed me, the bright eyes earnest. "I treated you well. He's the asshole who stole you and cheated."

I wrench my face away. "Cheated in your disgusting *game*?" My gaze darts from side to side. Nowhere to go. "You missed *that* tiny fact when telling my family why you wanted me to go to Reodian with you." I jab a finger at him, stopping short of his chest. Who knows what a dragon's version of 'not quick-tempered' is? "And you never told me three other bastard dragons were chasing me too."

He closes his eyes and inhales slowly. "Come into the house. I've had a long night looking for you. I need a drink, as do you."

"And my dagger."

He opens his eyes. "The others took your dagger? Hmm. Seems I was lucky that you didn't use that on *me*."

Cam guides me up the three steps to the entrance, a hand in the small of my back. His smug arrogance from our earlier time together pissed me off, and I wanted nothing more than to get away from him. But I spent more time with Cam than the others and despite the strong hints what he'd like to do with me, I never felt threatened.

"Take me to your city now," I whisper. "You found me first."

"I'm bloody tempted, but I can't," he says softly.

I linger in the doorway as he wanders inside and through another door. Panicking that another dragon might appear behind and grab me, I hurry after him. I never entered this room last night, one that contains a long table made from light wood and six matching stools.

I expect to see a stove or a kitchen but only see shelves lined with clear bottles. Cam takes one, perfectly circular with a silver cork, decorated with gold. He takes a silver cup from the shelf below and pours the clear liquid in.

I scratch an eyebrow as he hands me the drink. "Everything in this house is strange and doesn't match the island surroundings."

"The dragon princes' hideaway?" He pours a second cup. "We come here several times a year. Sometimes with others."

"Isn't that boring?" I ask. "There's nothing to do."

He looks at me over his goblet as he drinks then tugs his bottom lip between his teeth. "We come here with *others*, Ria. Females. For fun."

"So that's all you do? Drink and fuck? Because there isn't anything else to do on this island."

He chuckles at me. "Swim."

"Mmm."

"Or swim and fuck." He licks the liquid from his lips.

"Don't look at me in that way. I won't be doing either." I expected the liquid to burn my throat but instead the liquid slides smoothly down, berry flavors bursting across my tongue.

"And here I am thinking you found me irresistible." He tops up his drink. "Aren't you at least a *little* curious what a dragon's cock feels like to ride?"

I hold his challenging gaze. "Bad luck. You won't embarrass me with crudeness, nor persuade me."

But images jump unbidden into my mind—*settled on him, on top of powerful thighs; hands and nails exploring that chest and torso. He'd take over, fingers on my hips bracingly hard as he guided me, slamming that huge cock*—I blink away the images because the last dragon whose body was against me in almost all those ways is the one who assaulted me.

"Ria? You appear distracted." His *grin*. He sensed what I was thinking? Cam prowls forward and pauses until our bodies almost touch, lips slightly parted as he looks down. "I should've shown you that night. You were certainly keen."

"That was an act."

"Then you are a splendid actress," he whispers. "You pretended to become aroused to the point you forgot where you are and didn't notice a man stealing your dagger."

I swallow and step back before any part of him so much as brushes my skin. "Right now, I only care about escaping the dragon trying to kill me."

Long fingers settle on my cheek as he tips my chin with his thumb. "Nobody is going to kill you, Ria, or harm you in any way."

"And the Ebon essence?" I say, pissed that he's speeding my pulse. "Doesn't that anger you?"

His full mouth pulls into a sensual smile. "The dragon essence you contain does not *anger* me, Ria, just as mine does not anger *you*."

Addles my brain. Draws me towards the type of man I'd never normally allow to touch me. To a *dragon*.

"Is the liquid intoxicating?" I ask, suddenly fearful he's using something to subdue me. "I hope not."

Cam tips my chin higher. "No. Something we like to drink if we need to calm down; soothing but will not overcome you."

"I suggest you pour some down Vel's throat." I sidestep Cam as he releases my chin.

"Ria. Take care not to inflame Vel," he says.

"Because Ruby dragons fight with fire?" I ask sarcastically.

"Oh, Ria. Hope you never need to challenge him as a dragon." He takes my hand. "Please. Once we return to Reodian, you've no need to see him again. We'll retreat to our own courts. You've a short while to endure each other before we make our decision and leave. Perhaps don't speak to or approach him while we're on the island, and we'll request he does the same."

I nod. "If you can arrange that. Now, can I have my dagger and more to drink?"

Cam shakes his head. "Not yet."

Swearing, I pull out a chair and sit. "Then sit down and explain who you are and what the fuck is happening. How did you find Vel, for a start?"

Sitting, Cam rests his forearms on the table. "I knew that if anybody would steal you from a ship, Vel would. I picked up his scent and flew after you both but lost him, so I headed for Lightpoint ready to ask around the inns if anybody had seen a ruby dragon. I didn't need to—he was stomping the streets and I could smell his anger. We fought, he flew away after landing me an accurate punch to the head and once I managed to shift and follow him, we arrived here. You saw the rest."

I take another sip of the eye-watering drink. "You seem to be friends but also... not."

He rests back in the chair and stretches out his long legs. "We're four male dragons, therefore we'll never fully get along —we'd never bow to others without a fight—apart from the First-Born. And this challenge has brought out the worst."

"Then the First-Born are stupid."

Cam chokes a laugh. "Advice for you. Don't say things like that when you meet them."

"No. But they are. The war between dragons came from conflict between the flights. Isn't that what the First-Born are creating here?"

He drinks and pours himself another. "The elders ensure the opposite, normally. They're training us and the tasks usually involve working together. They're teaching us that we're vulnerable if alone. I'm curious why they've chosen to pit us against each other this time, but they'll have a reason."

"And you truly think the First-Born won't hurt me?"

"I wouldn't let them." He tips his head back and his throat bobs as he swallows the drink before slamming the cup on the table. "You, Aurelia, are as good as a Sapphire dragon because your father is one of us and your mother bonded to him."

What does he make of the fact Luin isn't exactly my father? "The others are more focused on my Ebon. Including your elders."

Cam leans across the table and my hand is swallowed up

by both his around mine. They're hot, calloused. And touched me once before. "I've had a taste of what you are, Ria. Connected closer than the others and, yes, there's a wisp of Ebon shadow around your soul but you're human."

He reaches out and runs his knuckles against my cheek, silver eyes intense. His teasing and rudeness has dropped away. Why? "And the elders would listen to you?"

In the following silence, loud voices grow closer, and I stiffen. Cam squeezes my fingers. "If they won't, I'll prove to them you're not a danger. I promised your family that none would harm you and, unlike that other asshole, I'm a dragon of honor. All exarchs should live by honor, and I hope the elders kick Vel's ass for his behavior."

I glance to the door, heart speeding in case Vel enters. "So do I."

Cam moistens his lips and his face returns to the familiar expression. "And in the interests of transparency, yes, I want to fuck you."

I blink slowly, not giving him the satisfaction of a shocked response. Is this dragon trait where my bluntness comes from? "If you think I'll lie with you to say 'thank you' for your help, you're sorely mistaken."

The door opens, and a hassled Eli stands in the doorway. "Luc's outside with Vel. He's agreed to sit down and talk but probably best if..." He waves a hand at me. "Aurelia either goes upstairs or leaves the house."

He's disheveled, a couple of leaves in his white hair and when he wipes a hand across his perspiring forehead, I see scratch marks. Such un-royal behavior from them all. And Cam? Such royal arrogance, telling me he wants to fuck me as if he expects me to.

"I'll wait outside until it's safe." Neither respond with the smile and reassurance I wanted. "And I'll take this."

I snatch the half-empty bottle and cup from the table and

stand. Tucking the bottle under one arm, I turn back to Cam. "Thank you for the warning."

"About the First-Born? You're welcome."

"No, Cam. About the fucking." I lift my head high and make my way to a second door at the rear of the building.

And leave.

CHAPTER 14

CAMANOR

ALL FOUR OF US IN ONE ROOM HAPPENS FOR ONE OF TWO reasons. Fun or fighting, sometimes both. The last time we sat in this one, we drank and discussed our task, each trying to figure out the others' thoughts and plans.

We also agreed that we'd play fair.

I guess we forgot that Vel never does, since the selfish brat always wants things his own way. He's in the low chair opposite, fingers threaded together behind his head and elbows at right angles, scratches on his face and chest almost gone thanks to Luc's healing help. Maybe I shouldn't have started the fight with him when catching him flying to the island, but I'm fucking furious that he cheated. Even though I never witnessed him snatch Ria, I knew in a heartbeat whose leathery wings flapped above the ship once I heard the distant scream and saw the pair.

Not only did Vel break our agreement that whoever found Ria first wins, but he broke our other—treat Aurelia respectfully. Perhaps hypocritical of me considering our first meeting, but how could I resist playing a little game with the mysterious girl? Especially once her warm mouth touched mine, delicious curves beneath my hands in that bed, as she eagerly responded. Now *that's* a moment I need to revisit. I'm partly pissed I'd told Devin to meet me at the house because Ria was putty in my hands, her body responding to me in wicked ways.

That's when I knew the girl definitely held a dragon's essence—the Ebon essence we searched for.

Am I also pissed that Vel interrupted my alone time with Ria on that ship? Stars, I could've had the girl wrapped around me by the time we crossed that sea. Is she as feisty in bed? I hope so.

"You're an asshole, Vel," snaps Luc before I can get the same words out, and Vel flashes sharp teeth at him. "Not only did you attack a female but the bloody female we're trying to take safely to the First-Born."

Vel barely said a word since he returned to the cabin— once I'd persuaded Ria to sit on one of the benches on the back verandah where they couldn't see each other. Now, he's holding a bottle of dragon wine which he's already drank half the contents of.

"And a fucking cheat," I snarl.

He swigs again and looks to Eli who's leaning against the wall near the dining room, arms crossed. "Anything to add to their insults?"

"An asshole and cheat about cover the bases," he replies.

"And you wouldn't do the same?" he asks. "How's it my fault if none of you had the balls to take her straight back and instead pandered to her whining?"

"That's called diplomacy and honor, Vel," says Luc. "Oh, wait. You don't have any."

Vel sneers and drinks. "I'm taking her."

"I found her first," I retort. "No fucking way."

"Yes, and I found her after she left *you*, Vel," says Luc. "And then Eli found us. We're at stalemate."

"Fine. I'll take her now." Vel makes to stand.

"You're not touching her again," Eli growls out. "What the fuck is with you?"

"Um. The bitch has Ebon essence?" He's interrupted as I swipe the bottle out of his hand. "What?"

"Firstly, don't disrespect an elven high lord's daughter, and secondly, the essence doesn't make her Ebon," I snarl.

He stands, meeting me nose to nose again as the old challenge sparks between us. "I heard you fucked her, Cam."

"What?" I splutter. "No. Not yet, anyway."

"If you do, you're fucking stupid." He snatches the bottle back from me. "You think Ebon essence can stay contained forever? Just wait until it explodes from her. *Then* you and the First-Born will wish you'd done something about the situation."

"Vel," says Luc in a softer tone than any used so far. "The First-Born want to assess the situation. If they thought this girl is dangerous, they would've dealt with her themselves."

Vel's sharp features remain sour. "How can they let anything live that has the slightest chance of releasing that fucking evil back into the world? Risking the flights' destruction again? The First-Born should've taken the mother before she bore a fucking child."

"Whoa." Eli grabs his arm. "You need to calm down. If Talindra knew you questioned her, she'd throw you into your court's wastelands and select a new prince."

Vel shoves him before sitting back down, sore spot now poked. "Whatever reward they're giving us for finding Aurelia, I want it. I would've fucking won if she hadn't poisoned me."

I snort, and he glares. "Brother, perhaps that's the fates punishing you for your deceitful methods."

Brother. We're all linked by the First-Borns' blood, but we're not family. Fuck, no. I could never deal with a brother like him.

"We need to discuss what to do to choose a winner," says Eli. "Something that doesn't involve fighting and causing permanent rifts between our flights."

"What? Like chase Ria around the island and see who catches her first?" I mock.

"Not who fucks her first because I wouldn't have a chance then," adds Vel.

Luc hisses. "How many times? Daughter of a lord—two lords. Don't debase her."

"Ha!" Vel shakes his head. "Well. Find a solution or I'm taking her tonight."

"Ask her to choose?" suggests Luc.

Eli gawks at him. "Much as I agree with treating Ria respectfully, she can't *choose*."

"Then what?" he snaps back.

He groans and sits on the edge of the table. "Cam found her first. Be done with this."

"No," shouts Vel. "The task was first to arrive at Reodian with her. I would've done if I hadn't been so fucking stupid."

"Yes. Why didn't you take her straight there?" asks Luc.

I chuckle. "Because he didn't want anybody to see that she injured him." He flashes me a look. "Ria stabbed him, remember?"

There's no longer a mark, but Vel swipes a thumb over the back of his hand and growls at me, all teeth visible this time. "Fuck you, Cam."

How amusing that he failed due to his own pride yet blames Ria.

But would she have used the same substance to subdue me?

"We all know, Vel. She told us." Our amusement doesn't help the matter as his ruby eyes fill with flame, the energy sparking around him. I shake my head at the others. *Don't upset him.*

"Do you think Ria still possesses whatever she used to drug Vel?" asks Eli

"I'm telling you, it's the Ebon in her," insists Vel. "One moment she was lying on me in the bed and the next—"

"What?" I bristle. "She was in *bed* with you? What happened to not fucking her?"

"She was climbing over me." I frown in confusion at him. "Forget it. But she used *something.* What if she harms all of us while we're here? Give her to me and we'll leave."

Luc blows air into his cheeks and wanders towards the small window that looks out to the front of the property. "Did Cam tell you about the thirty days, Vel? As I presume Ria didn't. Her court have given us that long to keep Ria in Reodian, or one of the flights' courts, and then her family will look for her if she hasn't returned. Ria will also inform them of any mistreatment. Therefore, we don't do anything else that would threaten diplomacy. Our task was to bring her to Reodian, unharmed, and Cam has also assured her father of this."

"And?" asks Vel.

"*And* stay away from her. Don't even speak to Ria because she won't stand for bullshit. We've all seen that."

Vel blinks, and then his mouth spreads into a slow sneer. "Then let's see what happens when she pulls her bullshit on the First-Born."

"This still hasn't brought us to a decision," says Eli.

"Should be Cam," says Luc and I smirk at the consistently furious Vel.

"I'm inclined to agree," replies Eli.

"I still think Ria should choose," I say as if I'm graciously opening up the possibility when I don't want that at all.

Luc groans and wanders away, returning with more dragon wine. "That's settled. Tomorrow, we'll all return to Reodian with Aurelia and tell the First-Born that Cam found the girl first."

"And then we can move on and stop the fucking arguing," adds Eli.

I choke a laugh. "For a few days anyway. Someone will start shit between us again."

"Not me," Eli says. "I'm happy to keep life simple and pleasurable. Especially pleasurable."

"Good point," says Luc. "We can celebrate our joint effort in finding Aurelia. I'm fed up with human company."

Vel growls at him. "Not a joint effort when it was supposed to be a competition and there's only one winner."

Yes. Me.

"I'm not accepting the decision." Vel stands. "We find a different way."

Eli groans and swipes a hand down his face.

CHAPTER 15

AURELIA

I'm excluded from the dragon's discussion which pisses me off but is also sensible. They'll speak about me as if I'm a chattel, no doubt, and Vel will not be polite. Both are reasons I'd struggle to hold back my opinions and temper.

I sit on a bench on the verandah, drinking the wine. How do they get all their supplies to the island? I picture dragons with massive packs flying by then my mind flits to the fact they're princes. No servants here—surely these princes are like human ones and have a full complement of royal trappings. How do they cope, poor things?

I'm sick of sitting here listening to raised voices and wondering when a dragon will arrive to accost me. I could take a walk? I'm assured nothing dangerous lives on the island. In fact, nothing at all. I've heard no birdsong or seen any creatures crawling on the ground, only the fish in the pool. Since Cam tells me that the princes swim in the pool, that isn't dangerous either.

So, I return to the shimmering water, constantly attracted to this place.

Although they've a bathing room in their home, the dragons don't have spare clothes. My leathers aren't clean but acceptable, but my tunic is beginning to smell and I'm acutely aware that a dragon's sense of smell is superior to human. I'm not stripping naked to put on a show for dragons inside the house and if they're occupied, I can wash my tunic. If any of them do appear, I'm wearing undergarments that cover me and don't reveal much.

Removing the offending tunic, I then kick off my boots I retrieved earlier and wriggle out of the leather pants. The pebbles dig into my knees as I rinse through the tunic, watching the tiny fish darting around in the clear water.

The water's warmth is too damn tempting.

A quick dip. Short swim. Float around beneath the early afternoon sun. Forget about dragons.

The buoyancy and temperature could be a giant bath, soothing away a day's troubles and aches. I float around gazing at the sky, squinting in hazy sunshine. I need something soothing after Vel's reaction to me earlier. There's no possible way I'll allow myself to be alone with him again, least of all he might rip me away from the island in his paws.

No. I'll heed Cam's words and stay clear.

I keep an ear out for approaching dragons, but nothing and no-one appears.

This island holds many mysteries and stories—and history to me because this was the place Luin brought Calla and the others to find the jewels containing the First-Born. I picture my family, and my heart suddenly twinges that they're not with me. And that I never knew the whole truth until recently.

My tunic dries on one of the boulders and I swim back, refreshed, and ready to deal with dragons. Well, most of them. The sand amongst the stones sticks to my feet as I climb from the water, white undergarments soggy. The tunic is only half-dry, so I locate a spot where the sun warms the ground, and the springy grass spreads between the pool and woods, then lie back.

I'm sure a dragon has seen a woman in undergarments before; I'm not bothered they'll see me. I *am* bothered that they haven't returned my weapon—unfair when their weapons are body parts. My neck twinges at the reminder. I don't think Vel bruised me, the hold only long enough to frighten but Cam's warning words remain in my mind.

After last night's events and lack of sleep, I'm dozy and rest an arm across my eyes as I allow the sunny day to lull me to sleep. A loud splash, followed by another, sets me sitting upright in alarm and two male voices shout and laugh at each other.

Cam and Luc.

They're in the sparkling water, ducking under as they swim, moving fast through the water before appearing at a different part of the pool. Bemused, I watch as they splash around like children, attempting to catch each other. Luc disappears underwater for more than a few seconds and my spine goes rigid when he doesn't reappear. Cam, unperturbed, continues his swim, lying on his back and kicking through the water, before dipping himself under.

Apart from their strange activity and impressive swimming, I'm distracted by the way Cam's chest glistens as the afternoon light picks out the water trailing down his chest, each time he stops to paddle. These men are all hard lines and sculpted muscle, their torsos and shoulders broader than any mans. Their arms could wrap around a neck and snap with a single flex.

Cam turns towards me, and I pull my knees to my chest as he crosses the pool, suddenly aware I'm half-naked.

As he emerges from the water, my gaze can't help roaming down to his taut abs, how the trail of hair leading downwards matches his sapphire, but I drop my eyes too far.

Cam's completely naked.

Stars above.

I avert my eyes but not before I've an eyeful of an impressive cock, although to be honest the length and girth make my eyes water at just the thought. Is he trying to embarrass me?

"Naked swimming with a friend?" I ask nonchalantly.

A laugh reverberates in his chest as he approaches, and I switch my attention to the grass.

"Do you mind finding some pants?" I ask, cheeks now heating from more than the sun. *Do not look up.*

"Dragons swim naked," he says and to my mortification, he sits on the ground beside me and trails a gaze across my damp undergarments. "Obviously you don't."

I've verbally sparred with this creature enough to know if I show the slightest reaction to him, he'll seize hold and use this for more suggestive and blunt comments.

But *fuck*... He isn't touching but the vision of him stepping out of the pool, drops of water streaking his skin as he licked them from his lips will not leave my mind. The man is blasting sex at me, overwhelming my senses more than I appreciate.

I push to stand, eyes still far away from his lower body. "Would you like me to *fetch* you some pants?"

"Left them over there." Cam points to the opposite edge of the lake, closer to the track leading towards the house. "Does my nakedness really bother you that much?"

"I'm not accustomed to sitting with naked men who I don't know well."

"How about naked dragons you want to get to know

well?" I don't need to see his face to know he's smirking at me. "You've already inspected the goods."

"I did not inspect you." Before this can continue, I stride away, ignoring my thumping heart and wobbly legs, pissed off that one sight of a naked man is enough to send my blood roaring.

I haven't lain with a man for a few months. *That's* why I'm reacting to an impressive male body.

Two pairs of pants are strewn on the ground, as if the pair took them off as they ran towards the water, a green and a blue tunic a few feet behind. As I walk back with the two pairs of pants in my hand, I'm relieved to see Cam positioned himself in a less... exposed position.

Fuck, those thighs. I've never seen anything like it.

"Here." I throw his pants and turn my back. "Where's Luc? I presume he hasn't drowned."

"No." A pause. "My cock is hidden now, Ria. You're safe."

I snort as I turn. "Safe?" The gray pants accentuate how his body narrows into a perfect form, the edge of the v shape pointing to where his pride and joy nestles. "I might not have a knife, but I can hold my own against male assault."

Cam's silver eyes grow darker. "Has somebody assaulted you before?"

I swallow. "No."

"Liar. Who?"

"A long time ago. Can we not talk about this? I just reacted to the words you used."

Every muscle tenses as Cam steps towards me again and he places a hand on my shoulder, an odd gesture since he's also staring at my mouth. "I will never touch you against your will."

"Uh. Very well."

"And neither will anybody else." His deeper tone rolls through my body, his heavy hand still resting on me. I've never seen a man look and sound this intense—even Luin, who would scare me sometimes.

"You should inform Vel about that," I say.

Cam wears pants now but his naked chest is at my nose height, moving rapidly. "He won't hurt you."

"I hope so. Did you make your decision?" I'm desperate to disentangle my mind and body from Cam's proximity, as my skin remembers his touch. Kiss.

When Cam doesn't answer, I lift my eyes and the intensely dark gaze remains. His tongue moistens his lips and there's a different aura that shivers between us. "I like your undergarments," he whispers and chuckles at my frown before dropping a quick look to where my nipples are hard beneath the cotton, then arches a brow. My breath hitches as he leans forward, warm breath tickling the shell of my ear. "I see I still have an effect on you, Ria."

"I'm cold," I retort and cross arms over my chest.

"If I saw *you* naked walking from a pool, I'd be 'cold' too." I grit my teeth against his continued whispering. "If you understand my meaning."

I step back. "I hope you're not 'cold' now."

"One kiss from you and I'll be frozen." He grins at our hidden meanings. "As I was last time."

"I hope this isn't your new game," I mutter. "See who seduces Ria and *that* dragon wins."

The smile grows further, wicked, cheeks dimpling. "No. But that comment raises interesting possibilities. Almost as if you *want* one of us to seduce you."

I pull a disparaging face. "I've no desire apart from to reach Reodian, find out why I'm prey, then go home. Again, have you decided who takes me?"

"No. Have you decided which dragon you want to 'take' you?" The more I glare, the funnier he seems to think his childish allusions to sex are.

Very well.

Biting my lip, I look at him coyly from below my lashes, before placing one hand on his hard chest. "Cam." With one finger, I beckon him to lean down. "I have something I need to admit."

He blinks away the amusement for mild surprise. Tiptoeing, my cheek brushes his—a mistake as this sends heat straight to my core—and I pause. A hand slides across my back and I seize his fingers, squeezing them. "I don't want to fuck you. Any of you."

"Are you sure about that?" he murmurs, his fingers tightening around mine.

He smells good. Too good, as if the water intensified his scent in the way the rains would bring richer aromas to the woods.

"You're not that irresistible," I whisper.

"Neither are you. I'm merely happy to oblige and never say no to opportunities."

These dragons need to know that I am *always* in charge of these situations. I slide a hand between us, running my fingers along his hardening cock resting against a thigh. He hisses.

"Is that so? Yet not even a kiss between us and you react to me like this?" Our cheeks remain touching, almost a challenge, and one I'm enjoying. I continue to run my fingers across the bulge in his damp pants. "Should I feel a sudden need to scratch an itch, I might ask you to help."

"You're wicked," he says, voice slightly hoarse and draws away. His leisurely gaze from my head to toes is like fingers on my skin. "And I like wicked girls."

More water splashes and I don't manage to check myself before turning my head to see Luc in all his glory too. Cam chuckles when I jerk my head to examine how cloudy the sky is.

Stars above, do these dragons have no inhibitions?

"What are you two doing?" he asks, his baritone voice curious.

"Making plans." Cam brushes knuckles across my cheek, and I shiver. "We have unfinished business."

"Hmm." Luc tosses a handful of small objects at Cam's feet. "We'll use this to decide, since Vel left to sulk again."

Stooping, Cam picks a couple up and weighs them in his hand. Smooth stones, shining in the flights' colors.

No. They're gems, a sapphire and an emerald as large as bird eggs.

"You went into the cavern?" Cam asks with a frown. "We agreed not to—we're unsure about the residual magic."

"I'm in one piece, aren't I?" he asks. "Ria? Am I in one piece? Did you see any parts missing?"

I mutter obscenities beneath my breath. "I'm sure the piece that all of you seem to value so much is intact. I'm going back to the house." Unless. "Or is Vel inside?"

"Wasn't when we left. Flew off to sulk," says the dragon whose cock I am trying hard not to compare to the other's.

"Good. When you've finished your games, I'd like you to all explain what's happening and when." I hope the pair don't notice how shaky I am as I stride away, attempting to be purposeful and not scurry.

They may not have an official competition to seduce me, but I'm suspicious.

CHAPTER 16

AURELIA

A CLEAR EVENING SKY AFTER A WARM DAY BRINGS A CHILL to my arms, and as I sit on the ground I'm grateful for the crackling fire. I'm confused why the men chose to congregate around a blaze because there's nothing to catch and eat on the island and dragons don't feel the cold—Luin would walk around in the mid-winter snow and not notice everybody else shivered. Eli lights the fire with kindling while Cam and Luc look for wood in the dark.

Vel doesn't return by sundown and as night draws a curtain of black around us, he remains absent. At least I don't need to see his face or experience his unwarranted hatred.

Cam and Luc stride from the shadowed trees carrying wood that yesterday was once part of a tree canopy. Large, heavy branches that look ripped apart by their bare hands—and possibly the claws they can summon. Dirt puffs into the air as Cam drops the stack from his bulging arms onto the ground beside Eli. He wipes hands on his pants.

"That should keep things going for a while." Cam flops onto the ground with Luc beside him.

"Shame Vel wasn't here to light the fire," I say jokingly as the flames lick the small sticks.

"We only use our flight's magic when shifted and when strictly necessary," he replies. "Usually. We can conjure magic in this form, but it's weaker."

"Do you all conjure fire? I never saw my father use any magic."

"No. Sapphire are storm dragons," says Cam. "I'd hit with lightning."

"Ice magic," says Eli with a smile. "Although we're healers too."

"Emerald have more healing than offensive magic," says Luc. "But we can summon both fire and storm if we want to."

And Ebon? I know this—shadow magic that creates decay and once ravaged all the lands. Magic that causes addiction amongst the Ebon elves who worshipped the Ebon Queen, caught in her thrall. My mother possessed this too, perhaps still does, but not through choice. She was pursued and threatened with death because she was born a Daughter of Shadow, yet she's the one who ultimately destroyed the Queen.

My fathers protected her even though they also risked their lives. Calla told me stories, but the men don't speak to me about this often, something they'd like to tuck away in history and not face the memories. Luin especially will cut short any questions. Perhaps my true origins are why?

"What's this fire for?" I ask. "You don't have anything to cook and don't get cold." I'm wearing my cloak and still need the fire's warmth; these men are in sleeveless tunics.

"The fire is because we need the stones to answer our question," says Eli.

"How?"

"Oracle stones," Eli says. "We throw them into the fire and whichever glows when the embers die is our answer—that color is the flight prince who returns you." He retrieves the stones from his pant's pocket.

"Then why not do that originally?" I ask. "*Then* send one of you to look for me?"

Cam snorts softly and holds both arms behind himself, palms down on the ground. His long hair, now loose, tips towards the dirt. "Because the First-Born are challenging our mettle, of course."

"You didn't bring the fifth stone," comments Luc.

Cam and Eli fall silent, the low spitting from the fire not enough to fill the sudden quiet. A strange unease creeps across my scalp.

"We don't need the onyx," Cam says softly. "The Ebon flight isn't here."

My hand tightens on a small stone beside me, and I avoid everybody's eyes—especially Luc's following our conversation yesterday. I almost—*almost*—comment that if we used the onyx stone, and that glowed, I'd win and could go home.

But the subject is best dropped.

Immediately.

"Will Vel accept a decision made by mystical stones?" I ask with disbelief.

"Either that or we fight to the death," says Cam casually. I spin my head around to look at him and he winks at me. "Just joking."

"What was the fight earlier?"

"Not to the death." He shifts to take hold of the sapphire stone, squeezes the round gem in his hand and tosses it into the fire. Blue flames spurt upwards before settling back to deep amber.

119

"What if Vel doesn't come back?" asks Eli as he repeats the action with the moonstone gem.

"He will. The asshole won't be beaten. He won't risk us taking Ria without him," Cam replies.

I tuck my knees beneath my chin and watch as Luc's gem disappears into the fire too. "How long does this take?"

"We'll keep the fire going until Vel returns," says Cam, and I groan. "He'll be here before the moon is at its height. Guaranteed."

"Before Cam drinks all the wine," adds Luc.

Cam takes long gulps from a bottle beside him. "*Me?* You drink so much nobody sees you until evening sometimes."

"That's usually due to the company I keep in my bed." He takes the bottle and drinks. "Not the wine."

Switching off from their banter, I focus on the mesmerizing flames, where the flight colors dip and grow between the amber, creating a deadly beauty. What are these men like at their courts? They're apparently separate but this camaraderie and comfort in their surroundings suggests they often spend time enjoying debauchery together.

"Do you own this place?" I ask.

"Vel built it as a bolt-hole for when politics pisses him off." Eli takes a slow drink then offers me the bottle, but I shake my head.

"You mean, when someone upsets him by telling him what to do?" I ask and Luc snorts. "Cam told me about your 'stays'. And the visitors you bring."

"Exclusive invite only to the island. You're honored," says Luc with a wink. "But mostly we come here as a group, alone."

"And cooperate? Do you fight much?" I ask pointedly.

Eli gives me a long look. "The flights aren't going to war again, if that's what you mean."

"No." I frown. "But there's tension."

"You mean Vel?" Cam arches a brow. "He's not usually this bad. It's the competition."

"He's a brat," retorts Eli. "Always was."

Hmm. "Sounds like a good thing you spend most time in your separate courts," I comment.

"Yes, but we're still united as a realm," says Luc. He nods at me. "Are you hungry?"

"You have something decent to eat?" My growly stomach leaps in hope.

"Just the dried meats and fruits. Sorry." He offers a smile.

"How do men your size sustain yourselves on that?" The meat jerky I bit into this morning salted my mouth to the point I downed three glasses of Luc's apple juice.

"We don't eat as often," says Cam. "But when we do, we eat a *lot*."

"Tonight, we have the wine. We're happy." Eli lifts the bottle.

The whole time I'm distracted as I watch the sky for Vel, the apprehension helping stave off the hunger. The wine flows down the dragons' throat and I'm unsure if I should worry about that too. These are primal creatures and I've seen and heard enough to know that they behave this way too on all physical levels. Remove more inhibition and... am I safe?

"Shouldn't you slow down your drinking?" I ask as Cam returns with several more bottles of wine. Last count, they were at eight.

Luc splutters and slumps against the rock he's leaning against. "You should be happy if we drink ourselves unconscious. Nobody will touch you then."

"Nobody touches her anyway," snaps Cam. "Or I'll break their fingers."

Eli snorts drunkenly. "Laid claim since you were the first to find her, Cam?"

"Nobody 'claimed' me," I retort.

"Whose bed are you sharing?" asks Eli as if it were the simplest question in the world. "We only have four."

"Nobody's," I shoot back.

He shuffles over and whispers. "Remember I said I'd kneel for you?" I give him an uninterested look. "I'm happy to show you some of my skills should you choose my bed."

With a huff, I stand, doubly glad I refrained from my love of wine tonight. "You're all very childish."

They all look at each other and snort laughs—exactly like schoolboys.

"They are. That's why I should win this challenge. Whatever the First-Born want to reward us with, should come to one with maturity who can handle power."

Despite my closeness to the fire, my body cools. How did I not see him arrive? Vel stands at the edge of the clearing, hands in his pockets, flame red hair more vibrant in the firelight. All his ruby features are accentuated, beautiful and sinister, made worse by his displeasure.

I sidestep so I'm between Luc and Cam.

"Have a drink, you grumpy bastard," says Cam and rolls a bottle across to him.

Vel crosses his arms. "Why the campfire?"

"Oracle stones. Luc found them in the Guardian's Cavern." Eli tosses the remaining gem to Vel who deftly catches and examines the smooth stone.

"And what great question are you wasting them on?" he sneers.

"The obvious one, Vel," says Cam, voice lowering to an almost growl.

A derisive noise comes from Vel as he tosses the stone into the fire. Flames grow as if he'd poured oil into the blaze, and I cringe back as the fire flares. Wouldn't the fire dragon's stone naturally 'win'?

Vel hasn't looked at me once and takes his place at the edge of the group, far from me, again refusing Cam's offered wine. My pounding heart slows —slightly.

"Am I to stay out here until the decision is made?" I ask Luc.

"Yes." Eli jerks his head to the fire. "We can allow the blaze to die now the fourth stone is inside."

I suppose a place by the fire is better than one in a cold room even if my company's behavior grows increasingly out of control. The dragons lapse into speaking their language and my eyes glaze over at the tediousness and tiredness, also irritated that they're excluding me. Not every word escapes my understanding and at one point they're talking about me —naturally. I also catch words Luin uses when he's angry.

Great.

But Vel says nothing, staring into the flames. I'm fascinated how the fire changes his features, as if he's a creature that's stepped from the blaze and took on human form, the color glowing on his skin and picking out the scarlet hair. At one point, he turns his unnatural eyes towards me, as if aware I'm watching. Refusing to look intimidated, I hold his gaze and we stare at each other until Cam interrupts him.

"This is taking a while. Are you keeping the fire alight?" he asks Vel.

"No. I have no desire to sit here all night, but I need to ensure nobody cheats," he says gruffly.

"Ha!" Eli drunkenly pokes him in the chest. "Pot. Kettle."

"You have to accept the stones' decision, Vel," slurs Luc.

Again, derision from Vel. "Why don't we just play cards or dice instead? There's no difference."

"The fates decide," says Eli solemnly.

"As with cards and dice." Vel pushes his tongue against his teeth and stands. "You've emptied your wine. I'll bring more."

My back goes straight as I again count the number of bottles on the ground. "How much can dragons drink before they pass out?"

"Enough to enjoy an evening." Cam leans forward and takes my face in both hands. Before I can pull back, his tongue runs from my chin to my nose.

"Get your hands off me!" He's lucky his face doesn't meet my fist. "Or I'll rip your tongue out."

Cam's breath reeks of the wine and his unfocused eyes dance with amusement.

I'm even more pissed by Eli and Luc joining the laughter, and I shove at him. "You asshole. What happened to nobody touching me?"

"Dragons often lick each other as a sign of affection," says Cam, poker faced.

I narrow my eyes as he chuckles. Even Vel fights a smile. "Is that so?" I snap.

Cam seizes Vel's cheeks and slowly pulls his long tongue along his friend's face, rewarded by Vel shoving him backwards with a snarl. "Aww. I'm apologizing for the earlier scratches, brother."

Vel confirmed my doubts. The dragons are teasing me. Eli's mouth moves uncomfortably close, and I prepare to retaliate if his tongue touches me. "I'm good at licking. You should try me some time."

His voice is husky and I'm well aware he doesn't mean my face, so I give a short laugh. "Thanks, but no thanks. You're a dragon."

"I'll be careful with my teeth."

Gods.

Annoyed that his wine-filled breath still touches my cheek, I shuffle away, my leg bumping against Luc's.

"What do humans do to show affection," asks Luc, voice now slurred too.

The two intoxicated dragons' thighs touch mine, effectively trapping me between them. Consciously? I swallow. Is Vel the *only* one I should be nervous around tonight?

"Have you ever fucked a human, Luc?" asks Vel, training his gaze back on me, as if catching my uncertainty about our situation.

"No." He tips the rest of his wine down his throat "I heard they get upset."

"Not all of them." Eli throws a stick into the fire. "Choose the right human girl and they love us. Trust me, I know."

"Even when you hold them down by the neck and they scream as you fuck them hard?" Vel continues to watch me as he speaks, and my body chills at the menace lacing his voice. "When you hurt them?"

"Yeah," says an oblivious Eli. "And I don't deliberately hurt them. The small ones can be delicate; you just need to be careful not to bruise their skin."

"Nobody is holding me by *anything* and fucking me in *any* way," I snap.

"Vel," warns Cam as he pulls out of his drunken state long enough to detect the tension isn't sexual.

"The Ebon never answered your question," Vel says softly. "How do you show affection?"

"We kiss. Amongst other things. You know damn well, Velanor." This is getting beyond a joke.

With another chuckle, Luc lies back. If he pulls me down to him...

Wrapping my arms around myself, I return to watching the fire, mesmerized by the unusual colors winding together. The dragons' fall silent, thank the stars.

Or not. Someone snores.

I look around and three of them lie on the ground, Luc

still clutching his bottle and Eli's mouth wide open. Asleep. My gaze flicks across the fire to Cam and Vel.

Cam is also in a drunken stupor, cuddling his empty bottle.

Vel sits, wide awake, knees pulled against his chest and smiles at me. "Finally."

CHAPTER 17

AURELIA

EVERY CELL IN MY BODY SCREAMS AT ME TO RUN BUT EACH muscle freezes me in place. I struggle to my feet, surreptitiously kicking Luc to wake him but he doesn't move a jot.

"What's wrong, Ebon?" he drawls.

"I am not Ebon."

"Like I said, I'm going to prove that you are." Vel pulls himself to stand and steps over Cam's prone figure to reach me, passing the dying blaze.

Now? "I see why you didn't drink," I say.

"The three of them don't know when to stop. Some of us have more self-control. Maybe you should thank me? Who knows which one would start pawing you."

"They wouldn't."

He cocks a brow. "You think a drunk, lustful dragon stops at licking faces? At least you know *I* won't touch you in that way."

My breath shudders. "Good. I'm tired. I'll retire now before they wake again."

Vel doesn't stop me from walking into the shadows towards the house, but with each step I take away from the dragons towards the cabin, I wait for a large hand to grab me.

Vel disabled his friends for a reason.

As I make my way to the verandah, Vel's slow footsteps move closer. "Aurelia."

Pausing, I turn and look straight into his eyes for the third time tonight. He's stooping so we're face to face.

Shit.

Go back to the others.

"You're clever enough to know what happens next, Aurelia," he says. "You have a choice whether to come willingly on my back or travel the same way as last time."

"Pick me up in your paws and I'll scream."

"Scream and I'll shut you up." Menace coats his words. "Unpleasantly, not by tainting your drink."

If I'd known the level of pissed off this dragon would be, I'd never have chosen to do something that stupid. "Vel. Sorry. You'd threatened to hurt me, and I was scared. That's why I put the powder in your drink."

"You're lucky the others were here when I caught you, because when I'm near to dragon form I don't listen to the man inside." He moistens his lips and straightens. "And Cam had already attacked me."

I frown. "Is this your way of blaming me for your behavior? 'I'm a dragon, I get annoyed and hurt people sometimes' doesn't excuse you throttling me."

"You think I'm looking for an excuse? I don't give a shit what happens to you." He jerks his chin. "If the First-Born have any sense, they'll kill you."

The ground seems to move beneath me. "They won't."

"I know." He takes hold of my hair and begins to wind it

around his fingers. "But if they see you for what you really are, they'll have no choice." I gasp out as he yanks my head back. "What would I need to do for you to let that Ebon darkness out?"

I wince as he pulls tighter. "Hair pulling? Really? That's what the little boys did at school."

With a sneer, he drops my hair and steps away leaving a stinging pain on my scalp. "I can do much more but need witnesses before I *really* try to provoke you."

His threats lash me and set my heart speeding. Cam assured nobody will hurt me and surely Vel will face trouble if he does.

But I'm increasingly aware that this dragon doesn't toe the line.

"I can't come with you," I say. "You agreed to the oracle stones' decision. Go back to the fire and wait." I'm blocked by him side-stepping as I attempt to pass. "Vel."

"My back or paws, Aurelia? Conscious or unconscious? Your choice."

"I'm not going with you."

Velanor watches me impassively and I'm about to turn away, believing he's dropped his challenge, until I see what's happening. At first hidden by the night, Velanor's body begins to change. Already, his arms have grown longer, muscle growing and knotting, and I fight showing shock as his skin splits, scales shining beneath. He keeps his distance as hands curve into paws, talons springing from them.

I swallow. *Do not show fear.* "I hope you have enough room to shift."

His face and head become unrecognizable as an answer rumbles in his chest. I should run but I'm pinned by that reptilian gaze and worried about those talons.

I've seen Luin shift but from a distance and only once— he hates if anybody watches, concerned we'll look on him differently. This close, Velanor's change is like something from a hideous nightmare. I cringe as his bones audibly snap and new ones take shape, elongated body swallowing up the space between the house and trees. Within moments, Velanor reveals his true self. All of his dragon—head, paws, tail. As the huge wings rip from his back, I finally back up, chest tightening as he stretches them outwards, the span now touching tree canopies.

"Fuck."

Velanor blinks, heavy lids over his glowing eyes, paws heavy on the ground as he steps towards me. I couldn't reason with the Ruby Prince in his human form; there's no possibility I can reason with the dragon. Even attempting to pass him to rouse the other dragons would likely lead to the unconsciousness he threatened.

And the teeth a hair's breadth from my face are much bigger and sharper than the ones he bared at me moments ago.

Would running into the woods encourage him? As if I could run far or for long. He rears up, paws outwards and I stumble on the steps behind me, eyeing his talons.

Back or paws. Conscious or unconscious. Your choice.

That paw could whack me into next week. I grit my teeth when there's no sight or sound of the others, their stupor undisturbed by Velanor's near silent shift.

"Conscious. On your back," I say in a small voice.

As Velanor kneels to allow me to climb onto him, I vow that one day I'll bring him to his knees in human form.

I hope the First-Born will be disgusted that he's won by dishonorable means and punish him instead. How fitting if the Ruby Prince's 'reward' for his so-called victory turns out to be one he'll hate as much as he detests me.

CHAPTER 18

VELANOR

EITHER THE GIRL FEARS WHAT WILL HAPPEN IF SHE TRIES TO escape or she's skilled at controlling her essence and didn't use this against me when I took her. Either way, the response Aurelia chose to our leaving the island helped her situation.

I don't believe for one minute that the strength of Ebon flight can be contained within a human body forever. That isn't possible. And what if she has offspring? Dies? The human who killed the Ebon Queen also holds some of this essence, yet the First-Born allow her to live too. Yes, they visited and assessed Aurelia's mother yearly and found the essence fading, but they were too late.

This human mother bore a child.

This child is now a woman.

A dangerous one.

Aurelia's family have an obvious reason to hide their daughter: she's demonstrated her Ebon flight traits.

Gods, how can the elders allow this to happen? A second

destruction of the dragon flights by the perverse Ebon flight must be prevented. An Ebon rebirth can't be allowed; the influence on the human and elven realms can't return. I've heard the tales told by the First-Born—witnessed the distress of the Ruby Queen Talindra. Our dragon matriarch rarely shows any emotion past anger, but I sat in a room as she wept and wept for the loved ones she lost. For the children torn from their mothers and slaughtered in front of them, as the Ebon ensured this was their last sight before they died. Men tortured and killed in ways I could never imagine and ripped apart by Ebon shadow when fighting in dragon form.

I don't care that the flights should be five again, not four.

I don't believe in redemption from such evil.

And I don't agree that this woman should live.

The First-Born immortals contain the original flights' essences and if their bodies die, they are reborn within another. Do they not see this has happened with Aurelia? Soon, we will *all* see.

As the First-Borns' Ruby exarch, I have influence but only over my own court. None shall ever hold the First-Born power, and all must follow their rule. Challenging them would be both painful and pointless. Influencing them? *That's* possible.

When we were called to perform this task, the First-Born pitted the court exarchs against each other for the first time. A trial of strength? Cunning? They didn't say, only that the champion would be rewarded. The elders also didn't specify rules. They told us the champion is the one who *returns* her to Reodian first, not *finds* her. I'm not to blame if the others pandered to the Ebon's wishes or fell into her thrall rather than bringing her straight back here.

My claws push out at a flash of disgust with myself. *I* didn't bring her straight to Reodian because the girl tricked me. Then she humiliated me. Weakened me. That is something I won't forgive, and the Ebon bitch will never find a chance to do so again.

I pace my chamber in the Ruby court, impatient to meet with the First-Born. I sent my chief guard to inform them of my triumphant return, and he returned with the news they'd grant an audience once the other flight princes return. I'm certain the three princes will be furious but if they put their honor above the challenge, and their trust in rivals, then they can only blame themselves.

The First-Born reside in Reodian, the central city and rarely stray from their place at the heart of our world, where the flights meet and trade. The four of us now work with them, given new duties in a campaign most dragons are unaware of yet.

One that will ensure nobody wars with us again.

The sun rises over my court, and I survey the lands. Beyond the expense and extravagance inside the court, other Ruby dragons live in small areas of regrowth or in the mountains a short flight away, some homes and towns hewn into the rock above the fire ravaged, still charred lands.

We suffered the worst losses at the Ebons' hands, but gradually, my realm heals from the destruction, with help from the Emerald flight who bring their powers to encourage nature's rebirth. The blackened earth that stretches between my court and those mountains now contains patches of color, where the first struggling crops from the early years now thrive, the rivers running again as the rains return.

Some mutter about the excesses within the exarch's court but nobody goes hungry nor are they treated anything but fairly. As a ruler, I must set myself apart and remind my subjects of the wealth and prestige that once covered our whole realm. From here, we can recreate our once glorious lands.

And no Ebon will stop us.

ARE THE COURT SURPRISED TO SEE ME RETURN, OR THAT I'M walking the halls at dawn light? Normally, only my closest servants encounter me at this time, if they disturb me in bed —either alone or with another—which is never a good idea.

Carrying a breakfast tray in one palm, I walk along the high-ceilinged hallway, across the white tiles inset with gold and red. The palace is cool compared to the heat from the ever-blazing sun of the realm, that's only occasionally replaced by storm clouds. Water is scarce here despite the new rivers, which doesn't help with the land's regrowth.

My route takes me from the royal quarters and through the center of the palace where guards man the doors leading into the building and the wide stairs opposite. In their silver armor and red and gold tabards, they could camouflage with the surroundings. I want the flight's colors reflected in everything, a symbol to others that none shall easily eradicate us.

I don't often visit the opposite end of the palace, where the guest rooms are kept clean and ready for any dignitaries that pay the court a visit. That is, unless the visitors are the other flights' princes who instead have rooms in the royal wing with their personal guards.

Currently, one of my guards is positioned at the top of the stairs, between the narrow doorway and the short hallway behind. Mal sits on a bench, legs stretched in front and an air of boredom surrounding him. Despite his Ruby parentage, the poor man has much-diluted Ebon flight blood, evidenced by his blue-black hair. This happens occasionally as sometimes flights would bond themselves to a dragon from a different flight and their descendants coloring can't be predicted.

Mal had a tough upbringing—I know that from how

others treated him when we trained to fight as youngsters, nobody believing he was anything but Ebon. Naturally, the dragon became a skilled fighter and is a valuable asset to my court.

What also helps is that he makes a good confidante and drinking partner.

"Mal." The arched door to the stairs closes behind and echoes through the silence. Interesting. The Ebon must've calmed down.

Mal turns his head, violet eyes not showing any worry that the prince found him almost sleeping on the job. He doesn't stand, merely smiles broadly. "Vel. Did you sleep well?"

"Yes, but I'm eager to deliver the Ebon to the First-Born. Any trouble?"

He shakes his head. "I never set foot inside, especially when she started shouting and banging on the door."

I purse my lips and imagine her fury, barely controlled last night when I dumped Aurelia in here after an unpleasant flight with her on my back. "Yet she's quiet now?"

"Yes." Mal gestures at the tray I'm holding, silver with a domed platter. "Breakfast meeting?"

"Of sorts." I sigh. "Unlock the door and stand guard in the doorway. She may've attempted to summon her magic."

"You think she can?" Mal pulls out a jingling ring of keys and places a brass one in the lock.

"With the right treatment, yes," I say tersely.

The door opens into a wide chamber with a marbled floor and smooth walls. Long gold drapes are drawn across the tall window, hiding the room from the dawn and shrouding the surroundings.

I suppose her kind prefers the darkness.

The bed barely takes up any room despite being sized for a dragon, and Aurelia sits cross-legged amongst the cushions, tangled hair spilling across her shoulders, still dressed in her masculine clothes. I eye the dagger sheath she still uselessly has attached to her thigh, smirking to myself that the poor assassin has no tools of the trade. She regards me, face shuttered.

"Good morning, Aurelia. Do you enjoy meats for breakfast?"

No response.

With a sigh, I set the tray on a round table close to the window and pull back the heavy drapes. "Time to prepare for our audience."

If Aurelia had yelled or thrown herself at me in a pointless attempt at assault, I'd be happier than dealing with this sullen creature. A quiet and calm Aurelia means I have nothing to work with. My boots click on the floor as I walk to an armoire and pull out a black dress which I toss beside her.

"You can't meet the First-Born dressed as you are."

Her eyes harden as she stares at the long dress, the silk material splayed on the bed beside her. "I'm not wearing what you tell me, asshole."

"Ah. You haven't lost your tongue."

The hatred in her eyes amuses me, as does her mettle. "Where are the other princes? I'm surprised they haven't knocked you unconscious yet."

"We'll see them at the audience with the First-Born." I lift my chin. "I would advise you to change. Making a good impression on Talindra could help your cause."

"What cause?" she snaps back.

I shrug before turning to walk away. "Who knows?"

"At least I won't have to see your smug, arrogant face again once they reward you," she says. "And I don't care who the dragon queen or whatever she is thinks of me."

I pause and my amused smile causes her eyes to flash with the anger I love to entice from her. "Very well."

What *will* they do with Aurelia? I don't believe for a

moment that she's walking away from our realm any time soon and certainly not before the thirty days are complete.

But one hint of Ebon and the elders will have cause to approach the elven and human leaders. They'll seek agreement that Aurelia should be eradicated, the essence recaptured and stored somewhere safe. Not within a body.

I'm not a monster; I have a sliver of sympathy that the girl never had a choice in receiving the Ebon Queen's gift through her mother. But that's by the by. She is what she is.

Aurelia pulls herself from the bed and strides over, before looking up at me. She's impressively tall for a human female, no doubt inherited from the human knight who fathered her, but she's deceptively slender. I haven't fucked a human and her body on mine two nights ago intrigued me, most of all because her ample breasts pressed against my chest and the sweetness of her scent dove into me, everything taking over my senses.

And the effect of the movement she made in her attempt to climb over *aroused* me. Oh, how the Ebon seductress lurks below the surface. Why else would my cock stiffen at her scent and images of her lying back and taking me deep and hard fill my mind's eye? I'm sickened that I reacted like that —what if I'm attracted to the malevolence inside her and this does happen?

Even now, her pink-cheeked, furious face holds a beauty I never expected. I picture myself dragging that plump bottom lip into my mouth and biting until she bled, and I will if she so much as tries to seduce me again.

"You devious, cheating bastard." Her bravado impresses me, but she can't hide her trembling.

"You're rather charming, aren't you?" I sneer and step away to pull the silver dome from the plate. Aromas of freshly seared meats escape, reminding me I need to breakfast too. "Eat."

Her tongue runs across her top teeth, shining white but blunt. No wonder she requires sharp weapons. "No, thank you, *Prince Velanor*."

Such venom in her words. I drop the dome back onto the tray.

Aurelia's interest shifts behind me, to where Mal rests against the doorframe, longsword at his side. "Is that who sat outside the door snoring last night?"

Mal mutters something, and I bark a laugh. "Indeed, he is."

"Why post him there? I can't get through a locked door and if I climbed from the window, I'd fall to my death." She wanders towards Mal and sweeps a gaze along his broad figure. "What's your name?"

He smiles pleasantly. "Malanor."

"Nice sword." Aurelia turns away. "I'm not eating nor am I changing my clothes. I'll wait here until you're ready to introduce me to your First-Born."

I click my tongue at her. "Very well."

"And could I ask a favor?" she asks, halting my walk to the door.

Turning, I fix her with a hard look. "Go ahead, but it's unlikely I'll grant you any favors."

"Could I be in the room when you're reunited with the other princes?" She smirks. "Mal. Are you a betting man? Who'll win if the others try to beat the shit out of Velanor?"

Mal's laughter annoys me, and I spin around, fixing him a warning look as I push past and through the door.

Let's hope that Aurelia's attitude remains when she meets the First-Born, and they treat her with the contempt she deserves.

CHAPTER 19

AURELIA

I'VE USED INGRESSES BEFORE—THE AUREATE COURT STILL hides behind magic and only those permitted by Galen can find their way through the portal from the woods beyond. Vel's portal to Reodian fascinates me. Firstly, because I feel as if I'm walking through a shimmering mirror and secondly because once I step into the circular room in the city, I find four other portal-like features. They're rectangular, floor to ceiling and like the one I stepped through at Velanor's court, arranged at equal distances. The floor in front of each one is tiled with a dragon crest to match the flight. Each one shimmers in the same way, apart from the one with the Ebon dragon tiles, where the space is pure black.

"Do these go to the different courts?" Vel nods curtly. "And this room is in your flying capital city?"

He sighs. "Yes. Obviously."

I scowl. "Excuse me for not understanding how your

world works. Is this the only way to reach the courts? Are those lands floating too?"

"No. Only Reodian was moved above the world in the Wars to protect what was left untouched. The portals between each court and the city are for convenience." He purses his lips, eyes remaining fixed away from me. "Our courts are hard to reach by foot and protected by magic, as your elven ones are."

Yet that protection wasn't enough.

Cutting the conversation dead, Velanor leads us through a heavily guarded gold-handled door and down a straight, narrow hallway. Light shines at the end, bright white, and for a moment I think I'm about to walk into another ingress. Instead, I set foot inside a city unlike anything I've laid eyes on, so fantastical I could be in a storybook.

The buildings ahead of us are unlike any I've seen before. Elven courts are incredible to look at, but I can't picture how anybody could construct such a place as this. Partly, I expected the buildings to match the princes' home on the island, but that looks like a shack in comparison. Several towers push high into the sky as far as my eye can see, shining silver in the bright sun. Other buildings surround them, with high-domed roofs, seemingly made from glass as the sunlight casts rainbows across them.

"How in the stars name do you float a city?" I blurt and shield my eyes against the glare from the surroundings. "That isn't possible."

"Not to humans and elves, no. They couldn't achieve such a feat." He straightens his sleeves. "Dragons are superior magically and physically. How else do you think your Ebon Queen held such a grip on the lands, barely touched by their enemies' armies?"

"Ah, of course, the dragons are superior to us lesser

mortals in every way," I say nonchalantly, and he snaps his head around. I flash him a smile and he scowls.

Guards again man the entrance to a gated area across from us, dressed in gold and white and with an emblem showing four dragons in the flights' colors wound together on a tabard. One has roughly cut blue hair, the other ivory and secured from his face, an elven style on a human-shifted dragon.

They eye me disdainfully as I walk through with Velanor and across a courtyard behind high walls with a wrought gold fence atop. Inside the small area, four alabaster dragon statues bow to a central figure—a female. Not a dragon, yet despite her sculpted beauty not quite human with horns atop her head. Her eyes gleam with rubies and the four dragons' eyes also match those of the oracle stone.

Including the Ebon dragon that curiously they haven't removed.

I stumble at the distraction and Velanor mutters something.

"If you're going to bad-mouth me, please do so in common, not dragon." I right myself and brush imaginary dirt from a sleeve when yet another thick-set guard stares at me.

Throughout our short walk, Velanor hasn't spoken again, which suits me. I'm keen to meet the other three princes and watch what happens. What will the First-Born think when they hear the tale?

My eyes adjust to a dimmer entryway after the blinding sunlight. This one leads straight into an identical hallway to the other building, but with a slight elevation. Again, painted dragons watch me from the walls and floors. These creatures really love to look at themselves because where there're no pictures, the walls contain mirrors in gilded frames.

Velanor's purposeful steps tap while my boots sound

louder. The next guard we encounter looks at me as if I'm a bedraggled mongrel, and when he stares at the floor I do too, convinced I must trail dirt.

No. The guard's face says Velanor is the one trailing dirt—me.

Velanor halts, just out of the guards' earshot. "Behave yourself in the throne room."

I balk. "I'm not a naughty child."

"As I am perfectly aware. You are, however, a rude and base human."

I've given up responding to his insults and push a hand through the hair I never washed or brushed. "Are the other princes inside, do you think?"

"We shall see." He smirks, not one jot of concern on his beautiful features.

Increasingly, the fact the First-Born queen is Ruby flight concerns me. Perhaps I should've changed into the dress.

An emerald haired guard bows and pushes open the double white doors for us and any bravado I had disintegrates. Four dragons sit on thrones, three male and one female. I don't even meet their eye before my spine becomes as straight as a steel rod. There's no warm greeting in the vast, cool room, only silence. Am I to avoid their eyes in deference or say hello?

The enormity of what's happening to me descends as if the statue outside had toppled and crushed my ribs, and I'm suddenly unable to breathe. In my early days 'working' on assignments, I'd hold my dagger, and my heart was in my mouth, each time scared I'd fail and die. I've never faced terror like this—not even under Velanor's recent threats.

If I thought the princes stood apart from other dragons in their allure, all would look bland and ordinary beside the First-Born. They could be the sculptures outside, they sit so still, skin paler and smoother than Eli's. All have long hair, the males' scraped back but the queen's perfectly straight and gleaming as if scared to sit out of place.

Talindra is beautiful, but that word doesn't encompass enough. Momentarily, I forget where I am, transfixed by her perfection.

That cavernous room amplifies what would be a quiet snarl from my left. Cam and Eli sit side by side in gold-framed chairs more opulent than in Velanor's quarters but not throne-like. To my right, Luc sits alone with an empty seat beside him.

Velanor's seat.

And Cam looks as if this time he really *does* want to tear Velanor's throat out.

"Greetings, Aurelia. Welcome to Reodian. I hope your stay will be pleasant," says the Emerald elder and nods his head. "My name is Kalinor."

The Ivory dragon beside him also inclines his head slightly. "Aelinor. And Delanor." He gestures at the Sapphire male on the other side of Talindra who merely regards me.

Talindra leans back in her throne, one elbow on the arm, hand beneath her chin, assured she need not introduce herself.

I stare, dumbfounded.

"Velanor," she says, her lilting tone matching her elegance. "I hear there were *issues* with the challenge."

Beside her, Aelinor snickers.

"I returned to the realm with Aurelia first," Velanor says, voice tight. "That was the challenge."

"You fucking betrayed our agreement," snarls Cam and Velanor's eyes remain on his queen.

"Interesting that three of you would work together," says Kalinor. "But unsurprising that Velanor chose not to."

"You want to reward the underhand prince?" retorts Eli

and bows his head, muttering an apology as Talindra glares at him.

The dragon queen rises from her throne and takes slow steps towards me, ruby eyes keen. Her gown matches her hair, low cut above her small breasts, midriff bare, before dropping to gold slippers. Matching bracelets wind along her upper arms, but she's no other jewelry. This queen is as tall as the male dragons, and the slender figure almost elven in shape. My mouth dries as I spot the small gray horns protruding from beneath Talindra's vivid hair and when she smiles, I can't help but take a sharp breath at the pointed teeth.

"Aurelia. Welcome." She extends a pale hand, nails sharp and painted gold—thankfully not talons.

Cautiously, I outstretch mine and Talindra curls her fingers around in a bone-crushing grip. Each time I met one of the dragon princes, their energy was immediately palpable. My essence recognizing theirs—the same one that draws me to them physically?

Compared to the princes' energy, Talindra's engulfs and surges through me, a prickling that borders on painful. All the while, she regards me and as her pupils switch to dragon slits, I fight yanking my hand away and running from the room. My vision begins to blacken.

"Hmm." She releases my hand and I stumble forward as the connection breaks. "Ebon, yes, but faint." Talindra turns back to the other First-Born. "Not an immediate danger."

Immediate.

I moisten my dry lips, darting a look at the princes who sit stiffly, attention locked on their elders. What does she mean? When she converses in dragon speech to her consorts, I'm both annoyed and worried.

"Why am I here?" I ask and cringe as my bold voice echoes slightly.

Talindra slowly turns. "Because we need to know how dangerous you are."

"I'm not dangerous at all," I say.

"Unless someone is her mark," puts in Kalinor and chuckles. "The little assassin is dangerous to humans."

"And would be more so should the essence consume her," says Delanor stiffly.

"I've lived with this... essence for twenty-one years," I say. "I'm good."

"Hmm," Talindra says again and tips her chin. "Still, we must address the Ebon flight's essence—their First-Born's very *soul* contained in a weak human vessel."

Soul? "You can't kill me." As Talindra merely blinks, blood whooshes in my ears. "Cam... Camanor promised my family you have thirty days and then they would look for me."

"Did he now?" says Delanor frostily. "And what gave you the right to do that, Camanor?"

Cam stands and bows his head. "I didn't want to fight the humans and elves for her, Delanor. You assured us no harm would come to Aurelia and so this seemed logical."

"And what if Aurelia is to stay with us?" asks Talindra tersely.

Fuck. No. "They'd come for me anyway, even if Cam hadn't bargained."

"And we would deal with that situation should it arise," says Aelinor. "Dependent on your condition and your choices."

"Condition?" My response is sharp.

"If the Ebon manifests, dragons aren't the only ones who'd want you kept away from the lands outside the dragon courts. Human and elven realms wouldn't want to risk you roaming free."

"And if I don't 'manifest', then what?" I ask.

Another tight smile instead of a response. Talindra turns

her attention to Velanor, still beside me. "You triumphed, Velanor. The one dragon who wasn't influenced by Aurelia. You apparently can control the girl."

I snort derisively. "By threatening and abducting me?"

"Velanor." Talindra's brows pull into a disappointed frown. "Is this true?"

"She is Ebon." Velanor's tone sends a new fear through me. "I had to take care against her dark soul, but I didn't harm her."

"Half-choked," I mutter.

Kalinor leans back in his throne and stretches his legs out, ankles crossed. "Rather fitting that a Ruby dragon won, my love."

"Yes. I suspected he would," she muses. "Velanor, your essence has the strongest control over Aurelia, hence you championed."

I can practically *hear* Velanor's smirk. "Yes. Is that the reason? You need the strongest prince to bring out that essence and deal with her corrupt magic? A dragon who can also control the woman when required?"

Kalinor and Aelinor look at each other and their subtle amusement doesn't fit the seriousness of the situation.

"Oh, no," says Talindra. "That's not the reason at all."

"With respect," Velanor says softly, "what is the champion's reward?"

Talindra appraises me and then steps towards Velanor. From the corner of my eye, I see his arrogance and cockiness subdued by this powerful woman. Whatever his new task or reward is, he won't have a choice.

"You are to bond with Aurelia. Wed her."

The heavy silence even manages to hit Velanor as I gape at this dragon queen, my heart beating so loudly I swear she can hear. No. She can't force me to do this. Beside me, Velanor is as still as Talindra when we entered the room, and as rigid. I side-glance to see confusion in his glittering eyes.

Cam's laughter peels through the throne room. "I wager you wish you hadn't cheated now, Vel." A familiar snarl comes from the dragon beside me. "I should thank you—I had a narrow escape."

I shoot him a poisonous look. "I don't want to wed or..." Ugh. "*Bond* with Velanor. You can't force me."

"Why?"

Talindra's simple question stuns me. "Because I have freedom to make my own decisions. I'm not under a dragon's rule."

"Would you prefer we killed you?" drawls Delanor.

"Yes, a much better outcome," says Velanor, loud and firm. "Or wed her to another."

"No, thanks," says Eli. "I prefer my unbonded life and you're right, I can't control her."

"Nobody will kill me." *Says the woman surrounded by eight powerful dragons...* "My fathers are—"

"High lords? Yes," Talindra says and waves a hand. "But not kings. I have spoken with the elven and human kings about your existence, and they agree we need to deal with the Ebon situation. Now, we promised not to harm you but also assured them we'll keep you contained. Your lordly fathers must bow to whatever decision the *royals* reach."

"We'd rather not have an Ebon vessel wandering the world, especially the one who has the soul." Aelinor jerks his chin. "Your mother has some of the Ebon Queen's essence, but we believe the soul passed to you. Not all Ebon elves accepted the demise of their courts and would gladly welcome back the powerful queen who blessed their magic."

"But I'm not her!" I protest.

Talindra cocks her head. "The Ebon elves who long for their old ways would take and torture you until the First-Born soul was forced to overwhelm your humanity. You are safer with us. Velanor will keep you restrained and when you die, we can take that soul and contain it again."

Restrained. I'm ready to vomit at how this creature believes she can dictate my life. *Thirty days. I need to survive thirty days.*

"How do I know that I won't 'die' soon?" I croak.

"Because if we murder you, your powers will unleash in protection. It's impossible to destroy the First-Born essences and soul, and we can't risk yours escaping. We'd rather wait for a natural death," says Delanor. "Things are a little easier that way."

"And we gave our word," adds Kalinor. "We have honor."

A dragon's definition of honor seems peculiarly unlike a human or elf's.

"You know that the Ruby exarch hates me and wants me dead?" I ask desperately. "What if Velanor kills me?"

Talindra slants her head. "Then he will lose his position as exarch, and we will exile him for going against our wishes. Velanor is not stupid enough to defy us." The spike of fear from Velanor is tangible. "Correct, Velanor?"

"Yes, My Queen," he mumbles. "But what of an heir? Aurelia isn't dragon. She'll produce no child."

"You live much longer than a human, Velanor. Once her human life ends, you may bond to another." Talindra pauses at my sharp breath. "Ends of *natural causes,*" she adds with a smile that does not make this alright.

This can't be happening to me.

I'm not in reality but instead a dream where dragons in opulent palaces, and princes who wish to gain more power, take my life and decide my future. What the fuck does bonding and becoming Velanor's consort mean?

Because if the First-Born expect anything physical, they're delusional that either of us are prepared to do as they dictate.

WINGS OF RUBY AND FLAME

Delanor stands. "We have much to talk to you about, exarchs. Once Velanor has returned his bride to his court, you must meet us in the keep."

Bride. The word bounces around my mind now empty of anything but sheer panic.

"The next challenge?" asks Cam. "Or has something occurred in the month since we left Reodian?"

"Velanor isn't the only exarch with duties, Camanor. Nor are your trials over." He waves a hand and makes to walk away, but beside him Aelinor chuckles.

"Del. I'd rather not leave the four alone in the throne room. We'd spend days clearing up the bloodied mess." He also gestures. "There's a little *tension* around them."

Talindra's mouth twitches into a smile. "I believe lessons have been learned. Haven't they, Velanor, Exarch of the Ruby Flight?"

If I weren't so terrified and pissed, I'd gain satisfaction at how Velanor has humiliated himself much more than I ever could hope.

But whatever the fuck I need to do to escape this situation, I'll need to work with this creature who despises everything I am.

So much for never seeing the Ruby Prince again once we returned to Reodian.

CHAPTER 20

LUCANOR

THE HALLS INSIDE REODIAN'S CENTRAL PALACE LEAD TO AN inner chamber that few are permitted to enter. Anybody approaching needs to pass swathes of armed guards which means only those the First-Born request to see are ever invited into their sanctum. The room the elders greeted us in earlier is used for most official business, and I suspect they chose to meet there to avoid allowing Aurelia into the room I now sit outside.

I'm fucking exhausted. Pissed with Vel but less so now Talindra has hit him with an unwanted bonding. I'd give anything to see that expression on his face again in the moment she informed him. I do feel sorry for Aurelia though and I'm unsure how the First-Born will pull this off without upsetting our allies. I rarely question them but forcing her into a bonding with a dragon—a *marriage*—seems unwise and unkind.

Maybe I'm too swayed in my belief that Aurelia isn't

influenced by the Ebon inside her. Or perhaps that's my attraction to her interfering. I never expected to respond to her as if she's a dragon but isn't that part of the reason we knew that we'd effectively find her?

Secretly, Talindra's grip on the flights makes me uncomfortable. As the only female of the First-Born elders, she's taken the other three as consorts and very much rules our realm. None dare question her and I sometimes wonder if the men ever speak against their queen. I suspect Delanor does since he's like Cam—filled with charm yet also cunning.

Cam approaches, a very different man to the drunken one covered in dust from the ground we woke on. We all had to be considering we met with our Elders, Cam back in his regal fitted blue and gold tunic rather than the looser one he wore on the island, scrubbed clean and wearing his royal rings.

He pauses ahead of me, and I stand. Hair pulled from his face, he's also less the scruffy dragon searching for the Ebon girl, and I know exactly why he's grinning.

"Have you seen the poor bastard yet?"

I bite down a smile. "Vel? No."

"I'd planned to beat the shit out of him, but now laughing at him will do as much damage. We should plan a night at the cantina and invite him. Take some women." Cam slaps me on the back. "Show him what he'll miss out on."

I snort. "The bond won't stop Vel fucking other women. Nobody pays attention to that bullshit anymore."

"The *elders* will. If Vel betrays his bonded, there'll be consequences." Cam's smug amusement grows as he waves a hand. "Vel will be the paragon of dragon royalty."

"I still say he'll fuck others. Nobody can watch him all the time."

Cam shrugs. "If he wants to risk losing his position. Vel's brother might live a simpler life at the edges of his court, but Sav can takeover."

He's right. Vel fucked up his life by trying to fuck us over. I've no sympathy.

"What do you think we're here for?" Cam asks and nods at the ornate doors. "We've been away over a month. They should let us take time out."

"If this is another challenge..." I groan. "No more walking up bloody mountains to the camps."

The camps. If the humans and elves knew the dragons readied an army again, there'd be greater trouble than half-abducting a lord's daughter. Captains naturally come from the Ruby flight, but every exarch is expected to rally the secret troops, hidden in the mountains only reachable by flying. A week living rough in tents was enough for me, and the others didn't fare well either.

Movement inside the room cuts our talk dead as a guard opens the doors and inclines his head in deference. I stride into the circular room with Cam beside me. The space is deceptively empty, chairs arranged around a circular tiled symbol representing the united flights.

What most don't know is that the meetings don't take place here but below. I turn to the guard, and he bows again and leaves the room. Once the doors click closed, we walk across to a smaller door to the left.

A narrow passageway winds down, this one carved from the bedrock and with no signs of the grandeur in the rest of the First-Borns' palace. The first time I attended the place, I worried the First-Born led us into a trap, but instead we stepped into a war room.

This place is dimmer, two lanterns either side of the door the sole light in the room, the room tight when we're all in here, dominated by the round table covered with a map, and the narrow seats surrounding.

The elders aren't dressed for an audience as they were earlier, but their attempt at more casual attire is equivalent to our formal. Even in my better cut clothes and expensive tailoring, I look ragged compared to the First-Born men.

Talindra pours over the map, an area that covers more than any other races' maps might, due to our ability to travel greater distances more quickly. Beside her, Aelinor stands arms crossed and eyes hard as Kalinor reads from a parchment.

Talindra's head snaps up, brow tugging deep as she flicks a look behind me and Cam. "Where are the others?"

"Late," replies Cam.

"Velanor may be entertaining his bride," says Delanor and snickers.

Her face sours. "I don't appreciate tardiness."

Fortunately for him, Vel appears with Eli beside him. Neither pay attention to the other and I suspect from the slight tear to Vel's tunic that they're late due to an 'altercation'.

"Apologies," says Vel and bows at the waist, Eli adding his too.

Talindra wrinkles her nose and sits in one of the seats surrounding the map table. "Everybody sit. Delanor. Explain the situation."

He nods and also gestures for us to sit. "We have reason to believe there's Ebon activity in the North Wastes."

Cam frowns. "That isn't an elven realm. And we've no need to worry about Ebon elves any longer."

"Not Ebon elves, Ebon flight," says Kalinor brusquely.

I jerk my head back. "That's impossible."

"That *should* be impossible," says Delanor. "However, the situation exists."

Eli rubs his head. "There're no Ebon dragons. Lyra was the last of her kind and her Daughters were created by magic, not birth."

"And they're all dead too," says Vel. "Apart from Aurelia's mother."

Talindra's face sours further. "Calla is no threat. We know that. We also know that Lyrandra had a consort—Cadenor."

"The elf killed him. Isn't that the story?" I ask in confusion.

Kalinor folds his arms on the table. "If one person with Ebon essence can be hidden, so can another."

"Fuck." Cam echoes my thoughts. "You think the Ebon Queen birthed a child?"

"Possibly." Talindra bares her teeth. "If so, we find him or her and kill the creature before they follow their instincts and take control."

"Or seek revenge for us killing their queen," says Aelinor.

"Their *mother*," mutters Eli. "Shit."

Vel sits forward. "How do you know this?"

"Patrols. Missing men." Delanor's claws extend. "No humans or elves live in that part of the lands. They can't live in the snowfields."

"Then this *possible* Ebon is alone?" I suggest.

"They can *cross* the snow," says Aelinor. "And unfortunately, will see our spies flying closer."

"Therefore, training our army becomes imperative," says Talindra tersely. "As does utilizing Aurelia."

"Utilizing?" Cam slants his head. "How?"

"She's Ebon," says Delanor simply. "Aurelia has the soul of their Ebon First-Born. The queen. Under our control, she can match whatever or whoever this is."

Vel abruptly stands. "You *want* her to become Ebon? Are you insane?"

"Sit and do not speak to us in this way." Delanor's voice grows harsh.

Sucking his lips together, Vel resumes his position at the table.

"Have you told the humans and elves?" I ask. The way the elders glance at each other answers for me. "The elves need to know so that they can send spies into the remaining Ebon elf courts."

"You know that they already do," says Kalinor. "Although most Ebon have turned away from the dark magic, there's always the risk someone may try to reverse that."

"And now this Ebon dragon..." Aelinor shakes his head. "He or she will be unable to pass through the realms without an army, so they'll create one to aid the Ebon's return."

A possibility that sickens my soul rises—one I'm sure that the First-Born considered. "The North Wastes. Many battles between the flights took place in that part of the realms. Many fell and their bodies never retrieved..." I swallow hard. "Surely not."

"What are you saying?" asks Vel.

"Bodies in the ice." I slump back in my seat. "Is it possible for the Ebon to create an army with those?"

Eli's jaw drops. "Reanimate? That's not possible."

A chilling silence fills the atmosphere as the First-Born remain quiet.

"No," whispers Vel. "*Can* that happen? Are the Ebon capable?"

"Possibly," says Luc eventually. "We're unaware if Lyra used such magic in her time."

"If she could, surely Lyrandra would've reanimated her consort after the elf killed..." This time Cam trails off. "You think this is *him* reanimated?"

"No. His body was burned with Lyra's. We saw to that," says Delanor. "Whoever this is either survived the original battle of the flights or is the offspring of the pair."

"And yes, I'm suspicious why this Ebon has located themselves where many dragons fell and were never afforded burial rights," says Talindra. Her jaw hardens. "I see you look at me as if we're overreacting—that as the four flights', against one Ebon, we're stronger. But this did not stop the Ebon destroying us before. Just ask the humans and elves who lived through their war with the creatures."

"Then Aurelia needs to know." Talindra blinks at Cam's insistence. "She needs to know what we require her to do. About the threat."

"No," says Aelinor with confusing nonchalance. "Nobody can know about the new Ebon threat."

"With respect," says Cam. "Shouldn't we tell the human and elven leaders too? Earlier, you informed Aurelia that her Ebon essence would lead to trouble, and you'd discussed *that* with them."

Talindra flicks her tongue against her teeth. "If Aurelia embraces her Ebon soul, she may become more dangerous and will be dealt with if necessary."

"You mean when you've *used* her?" asks Cam in horror. "Kill her? Again, you denied this would happen."

Delanor sneers. "Why would we speak plainly to her? Velanor has the task of subduing Aurelia if necessary."

Vel chews on his lip. "So, you're saying once Aurelia has aided us in destroying this Ebon threat, she'll die?"

"If needs be, yes, but I rather hope we can control her and avoid such an act." I suppress choking at Talindra's words. "But this doesn't mean you escape bonding with and marrying her, Velanor. We continue to assess the situation in the Wastes and must be strategic—not rush in. In the meantime, Aurelia needs careful controlling."

"Vel, we can rely on you to report back to us and not try to protect her," adds Delanor. Another reason they chose him? "And keep her subdued when we need."

"Although we must ensure that Aurelia reaches the strength she needs too," adds Kalinor.

"Hence, your next task will be to take Aurelia into the

Scorched Lands between the Ruby and Emerald courts," says Aelinor.

"You want us to go back there?" asks Vel, eyes going wide. "But what about the Charred Ones?"

Delanor's lips purse. "You can dispatch a few. They've been seen closer to the towns."

"The towns have troops," says Vel. "I ensure all settlements in my court are protected."

"Yes, but we want you to take Aurelia so you can assess her response in a situation she'd never face in her world. I doubt her mercenary skills would help against any Charred attack and such a dangerous task may aid in triggering some Ebon shadow," says Aelinor.

Vel mutters something and Delanor smiles. "You feel it is beneath you to wander the wilds, I know, but see this as part of the new role we've gifted you. I'd like you to lead the party."

Oh, great.

"Vel. We'll fly, kill some, and be back by morning," says Eli.

"Oh. No flying," says Talindra casually. "That would be too easy for Aurelia. I want her exhausted and behaving on instinct."

Cam's mouth opens as if he's about to protest, but he clamps it shut.

"You may fly back once you've completed your task," offers Aelinor.

"We'll be fucking tired *too* after walking for two days," complains Vel.

Talindra slants her head. "Are you questioning my decisions, Velanor? You are still in training, and following the conflict created by your last little task, working together against a common enemy will help smooth over some damage."

Trekking across the Ruby court's wastelands towards the Emerald borders will be excruciating enough without facing down the Charred Ones. These dragons escaped the war and now live in the scorched lands at the edges of the mountains, driven mad by thirst and hunger. They're beasts in human form, minds destroyed by starvation and unable to shift any longer. Thank the gods, since if they could their power would be unthinkable.

I've no doubts we can dispatch them, but taking Ria into such a situation... If Ria thinks Vel is vicious and black-hearted, she's yet to see a Ruby dragon in their state.

I'm with Vel—I don't want to go, but I'm keeping my mouth shut. Who knows what special task Talindra, or the other First-Born, might pass on to the prince who annoys them? Because 'gifting' Aurelia to the prince who pleased them was punishment in itself.

"And of course, we must prepare for the wedding," adds Kalinor. "We can attend to some of that while you're away."

Delanor merely smiles.

Vel does not.

Their conversation continues around us, and I barely hear any more. Our war with the humans and elves began before the flights turned on each other, and we could return to that state of war if the other races discover we've kept this information from them. The elves and humans may even believe we're planning on another war.

After all, we're creating an army.

And rebirthing the Ebon First-Born within a human.

CHAPTER 21

AURELIA

As expected, Vel's fury bounced through his own palace as we returned, the dragon not speaking to me as he marched me away from Reodian and to his ingress. I don't want to face or speak to him, but I need to know what this means.

Apart from that, I'm trapped.

The moment we set foot back into his excessively wealthy home, Vel practically shoved me at an alarmed guard and stomped away like a sulky child. Apparently, he has more 'business' with his elders. I understand his displeasure—I'd feel the same in his situation. Stars, I feel the same now.

The red-haired guard with the straight nose and teeth hesitates as he reaches to grab my arm. "I'm not running," I say. "Don't worry."

He withdraws his hand, relief on his face that he doesn't need to touch my dirty clothes, and I clench my jaw. I'm not a proud person, nor do I usually care what people think, but I need to be less conspicuous. I'm a mercenary who knows how to blend in and so I'll need to do the same here. That'll prove difficult as a human amongst dragons, but at least a dress would help a little.

The guard walks behind as I trudge up the stairs and through the door to the part of the palace I'm housed in. One small mercy is Vel's as keen as I am about sharing a bed—not at all. If we can't create children, there's no way anybody will know if we never touch.

Malanor stands outside the door, arms crossed, and his brow knits as we approach. "Have you stood there all morning?" I ask him.

"No. Returned a short while ago once news reached me about Vel's happy tidings." His mouth splits into a grin at a very non-amusing fact.

"And Vel will lock me up in here?" I retort.

"More comfortable quarters than the dungeons." He cocks a brow and the guard with me snorts in amusement.

"Dungeons?" I ask in alarm.

"No dungeons. There's a prison in the mountains."

"I'm not a prisoner."

Mal slants his head, and his pursed lips tell me otherwise. "Thank you, Dorn," he says, turning to the guard.

As the guards footsteps click away, Mal opens the door to my room, and I thin my lips. "Did Vel tell you what he plans to do?"

"Not yet. I imagine he *will* tell me. And I can guess." He flourishes a hand. "Inside."

A request not a command, although it may as well be. I cross my arms. "Guess what? Why would he tell you?"

"Vel tells me everything." He walks to the window and looks out. "You'd do well to keep your mouth closed and eyes open."

"Meaning?"

The prince's guard crosses to where I remain in the doorway and I look up at him, annoyed that every creature in this place is taller than me. Like me, he favors leathers and doesn't wear the white and red tabard the other ruby guards do. With everybody so well-groomed, it's difficult to fathom who's important and who's not.

Mal draws his teeth over his bottom lip, violet eyes glimmering. "As you can imagine, I've faced similar issues to you." He gestures at himself. "The Ebon features."

"Not only me. Devin—my father looks Ebon too, even though he isn't strictly one. That's where I thought my Ebon looks were from."

"Devin? He isn't from your family's court. I heard you were a noblewoman although..." He arches a brow as he brushes my dirty tunic. "You live as a commoner."

Every male dragon I encounter looks at me in the same way and creates the same hovering tension; Mal is no exception. Is that why Talindra wants me with a dragon who can 'control' me? Because I affect them all somehow? They scramble my mind too, but from now onwards I'll guard my tongue both against insults and information about myself.

Because I need to figure out how to get the fuck away from this place.

"Will you be my maidservant, as well as my guard?" I ask and poke my tongue into a cheek. "As I haven't met one yet."

His sharp white teeth shine as he smiles. "No, but I'm happy to help with any ministrations you require. Do you need help bathing and dressing as a noblewoman would?"

Is he expecting me to become flustered like such a noblewoman would? "I'm afraid you'll need to at least buy me a drink before I undress in your presence."

Dragons always laugh loudly—this much, I've realized. "I can request a maidservant if you wish?"

"No. I don't want anybody else snooping into my life." I

give him a pointed look. "I'm already unhappy that Vel posted a guard when I've nowhere to escape to."

Mal falls quiet for a moment, and something unspoken in his gaze crawls across my scalp. "Yes. You wouldn't be able to leave without help, so I advise you not to try." His jovial mood grows terse, and the creeping unease continues down my spine. "And heed my advice about guarding your tongue and behavior around Velanor. He isn't the easiest person at the best of times. Currently, he's likely to snap and lose his famous temper."

I nod, swallowing hard. "He can easily avoid me if he locks me in here."

"Not tonight. A celebration to mark the princes' return and for the First-Born to introduce the Ruby Prince's upcoming marriage." At least the smile he gives is sympathetic when I'm sure I've paled.

"Will the other princes attend this celebration?" I ask.

"Naturally." He straightens his shirtsleeves. "Have the First-Born arranged the first rite yet?"

"What rite?" I ask, heart skipping.

Mal frowns. "Perhaps they'll dispense with the challenges, since your bonding is decreed by Talindra."

"*What* rite?" I repeat.

"Vel proving his worth." He gives a tight-lipped smile. "As I said, this isn't a typical situation. I wouldn't worry. I'm more interested in if the princes can stick to their royal protocol tonight and not fight with Vel."

"Unlikely, unless they've forgiven Vel because he saved them from a horrible fate. I bet they're happy that he won the challenge now. Apparently, bonding to me is a gruesome prospect." I perch on the edge of the massive bed. "And I have no intention of bonding, wedding, or anything against my will."

The same uncomfortable look edges into his eyes. "Then you will need to discover how to leave."

Before I can respond, Malanor turns and walks away, not looking back as the door closes. The lock clicks, but I don't hear footsteps.

Mal remains at his post outside.

The Ruby Prince's eyes and ears.

I finally release the shuddery, teary distress I've pent up since standing in that throne room with Talindra today. Never in my years have I felt this trapped nor feared so much for my life.

The other princes must help me.

I swipe at a tear as my insides knot tight.

If only I'd focused on friendlier behavior around them.

CHAPTER 22

CAMANOR

"WHERE DID YOU PUT HER, VEL?" ASKS ELI AND CROSSES one ankle over the other as he rests them on the table.

Vel blows air into his cheeks. "She has a room in the east wing of my palace. And a guard."

He snorts. "Why a guard? Where do you think she'll go?"

When Vel doesn't reply, I tighten my mouth and pour another glass of wine. "What will you do about the bond, brother?"

"I'm not talking about that ridiculous fucking idea," he snaps back.

"*Fucking* idea. You don't have any choice." Luc sips on his wine and smirks.

"Didn't you fuck her already, Cam?" Vel asks. "Tell them *you* bonded."

I choke a laugh at him. "I did not, and you know we don't believe in this 'bond' bullshit. Nobody does anymore. Once you've done the deed, move on. Just don't let anybody report you to the elders."

"But *live* with it... her?" Vel bares his teeth. "I hope we find and kill this other Ebon and be done with her."

I grip the glass. I'm still reeling from the First-Born's news. They assured us before we left to find Ria that they didn't intend her harm but if they intend to provoke her Ebon soul, she won't be herself. I gave my word that Aurelia will stay safe and now the elders want to use her and have put the woman in the hands of a vicious dragon.

I watch Vel as he picks at his nails, scowling. "Don't hurt her," I say, and he looks up in surprise. "Aurelia."

"Not in ways you can see," he says nonchalantly.

"What does that mean?" I bat back.

"Didn't the First-Born say we should bring out her true self? I can make her hate me more and she can get in touch with who she is."

"Again, what do you mean, Vel?"

Luc and Eli watch our conversation silently, but I can see Luc's brow creased, too. Vel responds with a shrug and empties his glass in one long drink.

"If we face the Charred Ones, what will happen?" asks Eli. "I can't see how she'd win without her Ebon strength."

I sink back in the chair again. Talindra certainly enjoys her games. "I suppose we'll discover. But we shouldn't underestimate Ria," I say. "As Vel knows, she can be vicious."

"Without a weapon?" He sneers. "Shouldn't take long to subdue her."

Subdue. I rub my temples. "If we have to work with her, rein it in, Vel."

He blows air into his cheeks. "If the elders want to send us all on a 'training' exercise, fine. But when we hit reality, I won't be as kind."

"They don't want us to be kind, Cam," says Eli. "That's the point."

"And you're happy with this, Eli?" I ask and pour another drink. "Abusing her?"

He blinks at me.

"I'm not," says Luc quietly. "And I won't lie to her. Ria needs to know what's happening."

"You want throwing in the cellars for a month?" asks Eli. "Talindra would lose her shit."

"Ria's smart. She'll figure it out," I say.

"Are you sure you don't want to fuck her?" asks Vel. "She's started to trust you. Take her back to your court. Tell the elders I gave you permission, and we agreed *you* bond with her."

I lick the wine from my lips. "Much as I'd like to try her out, she's yours, Vel. I've others that I want to meet up with tonight."

"Tonight?" Luc frowns. "Isn't that the gathering to welcome us home and make the announcement?"

"And? Erinna will be there."

"She's with Sav now," puts in Eli. "He'd break your neck."

"What?" I purse my lips. We had a good thing going—she's voracious, which suited me. Lower born female dragons will do anything they're asked to keep their place in the royal bed. I think I cared for her too, since I never lay with another in the time people knew we were together. Oh well, onto the next. "There'll be others tonight. A dragon exarch is never short of a pretty girl."

"We could invite them back to the rooms?" suggests Eli.

Vel pulls a face. "I don't want to watch you fucking again."

"You won't," he says and smiles slyly. "Because you won't be with us—you'll be with your betrothed."

"*Not* fucking," says Luc with a laugh. He leans over and pats Vel on the cheek. "Maybe you can sneak off to get your cock sucked by a serving girl before heading home to bed."

"Fuck you," he snarls. "And who says I won't be fucking?"

"Good luck trying to sneak someone home," I say.

He stands. "Who said I needed to take someone home when I've a woman waiting?"

"Ria?" I frown. "But you don't want to fuck her."

He scratches a cheek. "No. But neither does she. With the right treatment, I'll trigger her Ebon."

"What?" I ask, voice hardening. "Against her will?" Vel gives a tight smile and turns away. My blood floods with anger and I snatch the back of his tunic. "You can't do that, Vel. You'd dishonor yourself." And *hurt* her. I swallow.

"What's your problem?" he sneers. "You don't *care* for her, do you? Did you get a little too in touch with your human side when we were looking for *Ria*?"

I'd argue with him that we have two forms and traits from each—dragons are not human, but we have humanity. Perhaps we're more readily influenced by baser emotions and behaviors, but we have empathy and care if we want to. If we lose touch with this, then our race becomes isolated again and from there the problems start.

I gave my word to another member of my flight that I wouldn't harm Ria. Although the words tripped from my tongue to persuade them rather than with sincerity, the more time I've spent with her, the more protective I feel. When I saw the dragon carrying Ria from the ship, heard her faint scream, I wasn't angry that the prince had stolen my prize but because he did what I vowed not to. Scared her.

I'd begun to enjoy Ria's company; the challenge to draw her to me. She bit back and females never do. Ria is filled with life that we shouldn't take. For Vel to even hint that he'd harm her sends a stab of anger between my eyes.

I've spoken to Luc and Eli, and they agree that there's

something within Ria; not only the Ebon but an effect she's unaware of. Does she know this could save her life? Because even if Vel denies the same, I swear whatever her power, it would stop him killing Ria.

But harming her?

"What's your opinion?" I ask the other two. "Tell Vel not to behave in such an abhorrent manner."

"I disagree but can't stop him," says Eli with a shrug, but Luc watches Vel through narrowed eyes.

Vel sighs loudly. "You don't think I'm serious, do you, Cam?"

The problem is, I do.

CHAPTER 23

AURELIA

I'M GRATEFUL THAT I WON'T REMAIN TRAPPED IN VEL'S room all day, but less so when I discover I've a second visit to the First-Born. This time, I begrudgingly change into a dress, plain black with long sleeves. Nothing I've seen so far about dragons includes 'plain' and I'm suspicious whether Vel chose to add black dresses to my wardrobe to match a certain flight's color. After all, the other princes', and First-Borns' clothes match their flight colors.

But by the time I stand in front of the First-Born, I'm pissed that I chose to change from my ordinary clothes.

For a few reasons, least of all that they appear to stand on a low dais opposite where I stand with the princes—in what appears to be a small arena.

I dart a look around and to the dirt at my feet. Is that *blood?*

Talindra wears pants cut tight around her legs and a snugly fitted tunic that accentuates her tiny waist, a long cloak pinned to the shoulders. In red. Always red. My gaze bounces from prince to prince—I haven't had a chance to speak to them yet. Surely, they can't agree with what their elders are forcing on me?

Cam nods and smiles sympathetically, whereas Luc and Eli speak to each other, only glancing at me briefly. Vel, of course, stands apart from them with his perpetually pissed look. They're dressed as they were earlier; at least I'm not the only one in unusual clothing if combat happens.

Surely that's not why we're before the elders, beneath a glaring sun, surrounded by a wall so smooth it would be impossible to climb. The only way to leave is through a narrow grilled gate.

Unease grows and prickles my scalp. Why ask the princes to bring me, then throw me to their mercy? I can't see any racks containing weapons, nor any discarded, only coiled gold rope shoved by a wall.

They look as confused as me. Is that good or bad? The other First-Born watch silently or look to Talindra, not at me. She has a pleasant smile on her face as she greets me from the edge of the dais.

"Aurelia. I want to assure you that as Vel's bonded, we fully accept you into our society and, as such, would like to teach you some ways of the dragons." Despite her warm words, doubt trickles through me. "We've organized an official ceremony to announce the betrothal tonight, but we have a rite the flight prince must perform."

Vel's eyes go wide, and Cam straightens. "*That's* why we're here?" he asks. "I thought this pertained to our conversation earlier about Ria."

"Yes. Vel's dominion over Aurelia is obviously more important than usual," says Delanor.

"Dominion?" I blurt.

"And he must show his prowess and commitment to defending the mate chosen for him."

Mate. *Mate*. That's the first time anybody used the word, and the connotations make me want to heave. Bonded. Bride. However, they dress this up, they're forcing me into something I will *not* do.

Quiet blankets us and my pulse races. If the princes don't know what's planned, this isn't good.

Dominion.

Defend.

"We don't need to do this. Haven't we already competed for Ria?" asks Luc.

"Excuse me?" I say. "What the fuck is happening now?"

Aelinor crosses his arms. "When dragon princes choose their female to bond with, we need to ensure that he will protect her at all costs. That he is *strong* enough to do so."

"But this isn't a typical situation," protests Vel. "I didn't choose her."

"Yes, which is why we're doing this less *publicly*, Vel. But should you protest—any of you—we can make this an official spectacle," adds Talindra.

The bewilderment in the dragons' eyes increases my panic by the minute. "Tell me what you're going to do." Attempting to climb that wall suddenly becomes a desperate option.

"Vel must retrieve and protect you from the other princes," explains Kalinor. "Otherwise, he's not viewed as powerful enough to take you as his bonded."

"This is ridiculous," says Luc. "Why would we fight him for Ria when none of us wants her?"

I choke a laugh. "Then naturally Vel will succeed," I say. "If nobody wants to fight for me or whatever in the gods' name this is."

"This is pointless," says Vel. "You're forcing me into a marriage and bonding that's set in stone, whether I win or lose the rite. I've no desire for her. I don't care if anybody hurts Ria; they can do whatever they want."

Talindra steps from the dais and takes slow steps across the space, eyes fixed on Vel's. "Exactly."

My head spins with confusion. "You're making no sense."

I twist my head to Cam. He said nobody would hurt me. Are these creatures asking the princes to do exactly that? And why has Talindra's comment shifted Vel's mood, and he's smirking at me?

A thought hits me like a bolt of lightning to the head. They want to provoke my Ebon, as Vel promised he always would.

But still, I'm confused. Are they *all* about to attack me? Even Cam?

"Each of the princes will attempt to remove you from this arena. Velanor must stop them." I shake my head at Talindra's words. Why create more conflict between the four?

"And if one of them removes me?" I ask.

"Then Velanor is not a worthy prince," says Aelinor. "Not only does he lose his bride but his position. You will be given to the prince who bests him and Velanor will be removed from court."

"And if *I* win?" I retort.

The First-Born smiles down at me as if I'm a child. "Against four dragons. Sweet girl..." Delanor shakes his head.

"You won't win," growls Vel.

"But you don't want to bond with me."

"I certainly don't want to lose my fucking throne," he snaps back.

Aelinor sighs. "Exarchs. Treat this as a rite you all need to complete. Go through the motions and let Velanor overcome you one by one. Then Velanor can tie Aurelia up and retreat."

"What?" I half-shout. "*Tie me up*?"

"Don't worry, the binding is only symbolic," says Delanor.

172

"The prince's final proof that not only can he best any who threaten his bride but can also never be beaten by the female. That she will always acquiesce."

Vel's smirk grows as he's given permission to *not* be gentle with me. I swallow down the hard lump in my throat. *Cam. Luc. Please help me.*

Sweat pools along my back as Talindra steps back up to join her consorts in a row. "I don't have a weapon *or* fighting attire."

"Hmm." Aelinor steps forward and throws a dagger to the ground at my feet; I immediately lean down to snatch my weapon. *Dragonsbane. Ha.*

"What the fuck?" snarls Vel.

"You'll need to disarm her too, Velanor." Talindra flicks her tongue against her teeth. "Did you think we'd make this easy?"

"You're all mad!" I say, picturing myself with broken bones from the dragons.

Cam steps forward. "With respect, Talindra, Ria isn't a dragon and could get hurt. I gave Luinor my word that Ria would come to no harm."

"She is an assassin. The girl has a dagger," says Delanor.

Cam looks to his First-Born. "Isn't it enough that we've created this bond without consent by either party? I'm appealing to you to rethink."

"Like I said before, Cam. You take her," says Vel. "For once in our lives, I'll allow you to beat me."

Cam's expression blackens, the silver eyes glowing. "That's not possible; Talindra has spoken, and we must do as the elders say."

Luc walks forward and pokes Vel in the chest. "Looks as if we're given the chance to beat the crap out of you after all."

Vel lowers his voice. "I'm not attacking you. I've no desire to fight. Just yield to me."

My fingers tremble around the dagger in my hand, and I look down at the restrictive dress. As a child, Calla taught me something that amused me at the time, a skill I've used several times before. Snatching the skirts of my dress, I twist and tie them until they're between my legs as makeshift pants. I've now naked legs, but at least I have freedom to move.

Delanor laughs loudly, and Cam nods at me, Luc winking. Vel grunts something beneath his breath and steps forward.

"Untie that and have some decorum," he spits.

I blink at him. "No."

His jaw sets hard. "Neither of us want this marriage, but in public you have to behave."

My laugh bounces around. "No."

I shrink back as Vel's nose almost touches mine. "If we weren't in public, I'd fucking punish you for that."

"Someone has a high opinion of himself," I retort, and step back. A quick glance at his hand adds more panic. I turn to Talindra. "The dragons can't shift for this rite, can they?"

"No. Not the first time."

First time?

Vel sneers at me and steps away. "Good luck, Ebon. I'll try not to tie you too tightly."

CHAPTER 24

AURELIA

Dragons are brutal creatures, and they don't pretend otherwise.

But Luin has a gentler side, and I'd deluded myself that the princes perhaps weren't *all* brutes. But beneath their finery and beauty, the dragon's nature is darker than any Ebon that they claim not to resemble.

The First-Born are fucking enjoying this.

And I think the princes are too.

If I could find my way out of this arena, I'd run. At least there's nobody sitting in the tiered seating that surrounds the area to watch dragons assault me. I'm shaking with adrenaline as I slide the dagger into my boot—I don't want Vel or the others disarming me the first chance they get. I'm on the verge of vomiting and consider doing so on Talindra's shoes.

I'm shocked that Talindra could follow rituals that show women as weak and as possessions when she holds the most power here. The queen holds too much power if these princes would do exactly what they're told for fear they'll lose their thrones. Or are they scared of something worse?

At first, I'm circled by Luc, Cam, and Eli, their backs to me as they focus on Vel. I can't move, trapped in the middle of three bodies who dwarf me, engulfed by the heat and the scent they all share. Nobody speaks and moments later Vel hauls Eli away and the other two close around until I'm unable to see what's happening, one in front, one behind. Their muscular forms press harder against me, and my breath quickens with a sense that they're protecting me.

My mind retreats as if I'm in a dark dream, half-smothered by these two dragons. Under less worrying circumstances, I'd consider being squashed between them not *entirely* unpleasant, their masculinity and the dragon essence having the usual effect.

"What's going to happen to me?" I ask in a shaky voice.

Cam's arm snakes around my waist and holds me to him. "Vel will fight us one by one until you're left unprotected. Then he'll tie you up. The ropes are over there."

"Ropes?" I ask, voice rising in pitch.

Snarling and shouting bounce around us and the thuds on the ground must hurt someone a lot. "Why is Eli fighting back and now allowing Vel to beat him?" mutters Luc.

"Eli doesn't want to look weak in front of his flight's elder," says Cam. "And he probably wants revenge for the other night."

I'm flush against Cam's body, the proprietary arm around my waist tight. "But tie me up?" I ask hoarsely. "Will Vel hurt me?"

Cam nudges his nose into my hair. "Remember, Vel wants to provoke your Ebon."

"Is that 'yes'?" I swallow hard.

"I won't let him." I shiver as his nose touches my neck. "I

176

can't be with you if you're in his court, but while I *am* in your presence, he should take care."

"What are you whispering about?" asks Luc.

"Nothing," replies Cam.

The sound of fighting abruptly stops and I hear Eli swearing furiously at Vel. Moments later, I'm jostled as Vel collides with Luc and his back hits my chest. Luc keeps his footing, and the pair move to one side, me stumbling over Cam's feet. The dagger's blade warms against my ankle where I shoved it into my boot. Prince or not, if Vel hurts me, I'll use this on him.

Cam's continued hold on me becomes annoying, and I open my mouth to speak just as Luc is wrenched forward and thrown across the ground by Vel.

I barely get to see anything before the pair becomes a tumble of limbs on the arena floor, each trying to best the other, punches thrown as they fight for the upper hand, rolling across the dirt. When Luc leaps to his feet and runs, my mouth drops open in shock as he launches himself off the ground and slams his feet into Vel's chest. Vel staggers backwards and sprawls onto the ground. These men have unusual powers in this form too. Vel's on his feet in moments, talons drawn.

Aelinor laughs loudly, and Cam swears in my ear. "Luc, back down," he shouts. "There's no point in this."

Luc turns pale eyes to us, pupils slit, talons of his own emerging. Taking advantage of the distraction, Vel slams himself into Luc and the pair sprawl on the floor again.

This is insane. If Talindra already decided that Vel and I will bond, why put them through this? To test obedience? Cause a rift?

"I'm sorry," whispers Cam in my ear. "Trust me."

"What do you mean you're—" Before I can finish, I'm

upside down across Cam's shoulder, unable to move as he holds my legs tight against him. "What the fuck, Cam?"

"Vel!" he shouts. "I'm taking her now."

"Taking me where? Cam. What's happening?"

Vel spins around, face streaked by blood, and my teeth rattle in my head as Cam moves at speed towards the gate. Hope rises that he'll take me through, but Cam sets me on my feet and turns my back to his chest, trapping my arms behind me and between us, fingers circling my throat.

"Camanor!" shouts Delanor. "No."

Vel strides purposefully towards us, his feral state intensified by the blood and red of his eyes, and I half-choke at the pressure growing on my windpipe.

"Don't be fucking ridiculous," snarls out Vel.

"The Ruby flight exarch is not worthy," announces Cam, eyes fixed on Vel, whose short breaths come as growls. "I challenge him."

To what?

"Camanor, release Aurelia," shouts Delanor.

"You talk of tradition and bonds?" Cam moves until I'm facing the First-Born, eyes watering from the sting of claws on my throat. "He isn't worthy. I've already won."

"You fucking cheat!" shouts Vel, only for Cam to laugh in response. "You're supposed to wait until I've bested everybody else. I was still dealing with Luc."

"Mmm." He squeezes my throat. "I'm taking her."

"You are *not*!" shouts Talindra. "This is a formality. You can't. I will not have Velanor removed from the court because you challenged him and won."

"Then he'll need to beat me without injuring Ria."

"You're hurting me," I rasp out.

"Not as much as he will if he gets his hands on you—and then what? You become what they want?" hisses Cam. "Trust me."

"Don't do this." Vel's low voice is laced with fury. "We agreed."

"Oh? And you always keep agreements?" He laughs, then lowers his voice again. "I'm going to let you go. Vel is going to tear into me. You figure out how to stop him from beating me and turning on you."

"What are you saying?" snarls Vel.

"I'm telling your bride how I'll use the ropes to tie her up and fuck her when I claim her as mine." His other hand moves along my body, and I tense when his fingers splay across my belly. "You said you didn't want Ria—perhaps I want to be the one to control her and prove to the elders that I'm worth more than you."

"No!" yells Talindra. "This is a *formality*. Do not invoke this right to challenge."

"Cam. Don't shame your flight," snarls Delanor. "Talindra chose. We do not challenge."

"Challenge Vel and you challenge me," says Talindra coldly.

"Then why even *do* this?" I look to Luc as he speaks, sitting against the wall, lacerated, and blood streaking across his face.

"Because it is a rite all must go through!" she snaps. "But you were supposed to go through the motions and let Vel win, not behave like this."

This situation. Their behavior, as if I'm something belonging to them that can be shuffled from person to person. Trapped by dragons who'll do who knows what to me. The fury and fear build made worse because I can't reach my dagger. I don't care what Cam is trying to do; even if he's trying to help, I'll still walk out of this situation with no choices. I've no control.

Then I sense what these dragons want. The darkness from the dreams, a kernel in my soul with the desire to hurt.

To conquer. I've felt this once before, the day two of Devin's guild tried to rape me.

The night that happened, a green glow had grown around my fingers and something like a tether wrapped around my hand as fear became fury. Amongst the dark magic coming from me, I'd screamed, knowing Devin was in the house. He'd walked in to find me breaking the men's minds, one's nose and eyes already bleeding. Devin took one look at my ripped tunic and finished him off. Both of them.

But I was barely in that room and hardly with the world, my only desire to pull them apart. I was ready to walk downstairs into the house and find *every* man to pull apart. Devin slapped me out of it, and I was so shocked that he raised a hand to me, shouting at me to stop, that I snapped back to reality. Whatever exists inside, I could never hurt him. The man who'd unconditionally loved and protected me. My father.

Or I thought he was.

We never spoke of that night again, even when I questioned Devin. All he said was that the assault had caused me to hallucinate in some way and that he'd killed the men.

Now I think he killed them partly so neither man could tell others what they witnessed.

And that darkness simmers now.

"Cam," I rasp.

If only I could see my hands. To know if the surging in my blood has manifested.

"Fuck, Ria. Don't," he whispers, still eyeing Vel. "I'm sorry that I'm scaring you, but believe that you are safe. I'll fight on your behalf. Please don't listen to what's calling you."

"I can't," I choke out as his grip on my neck loosens. "I have to fight back."

The fury floods my veins, hot and burning with something more. I close my eyes, ready to accept the whispers—protect myself at all costs—when Cam jerks my arm and spins me to face him.

"No, Ria," he whispers and seizes my cheeks.

I half-shout against his mouth as he kisses me, his grip on my face painful as he forces his tongue between my lips, claiming me in front of everybody. Instantly, the shock knocks away the magic as Devin's slap did, as if Cam's kiss surrounded the magic with a crackling energy and absorbed it.

Storm dragon.

Seconds later, someone else grabs me around the waist and tears me from Cam, and I land heavily on the ground. This time the blackness comes from the knock to my head and I watch Vel as he slashes at Cam, Cam parrying with his forearm against Vel's.

I crawl onto my hands and knees, then to my feet, looking at Vel's back and considering using the dagger in my boot. But a single stab did nothing to Vel and if I injure him badly, I'll be in more trouble than any violent rite.

Everybody else watches the chaos as I stagger towards the rope left in the corner for Vel to use. Another flash of anger and I seize hold, spinning around to where Vel now kneels over and pummels Cam.

Vel who stops abruptly when I spring to kneel behind and hold the rope taut before pressing against his throat. Vel's hands go to the ropes, as he tries to pull them away and he snarls.

"If this rope is for use on a dragon, I presume it would be too hard for *you* to break." I yank tighter.

"Ria," says Cam in horror, struggling to sit. "Bad idea."

"Not as bad as the alternative," I growl at Cam. "Right?"

Vel bucks, knocking air from my lungs, but I keep the rope around his neck as we roll on the ground. "Get the fuck off me, Aurelia."

"Beat the crap out of your friends if you want, but you're not hurting me."

As I pull tighter, he makes a strangled noise. "You wouldn't."

"Try me," I whisper against his ear. "I know how to garrote someone, and I also know when to stop. I'll choke you unconscious."

"You fucking do, and you'll regret it." His hands continue to claw at the ligature around his neck.

Someone digs claws into my hand until I drop the rope, and I scream out in frustration as the dragon takes away my ability to fight for myself, again.

"Ria. You've made a huge mistake," says Luc, pulling me against him. "Get away from Vel."

I don't see Vel's face until he manages to rise to his feet and turn, skin cut and reddened by both my assault and his fights with the others. I shrink back against Luc's chest, wrapped in his protective arms, but Vel doesn't move. Slowly, he circles his tongue around his lips and flicks his eyes away from me towards Luc.

Then he turns to Cam. "The plan I mentioned earlier?" His voice is guttural; inhuman. "That's how tonight ends."

Dragging a hand through his hair, he glares at me before storming away.

Cautiously I look over to the First-Born, all watching with open mouths—apart from Talindra, whose smile pulls her pretty features into something much more malevolent.

Cam sits on the floor with his head in his hands.

What the fuck have I done?

CHAPTER 25

AURELIA

THE WORLD CONTINUES TO EXIST BEHIND A HAZY BARRIER of shock as I sit on one of the seats that look over the arena, Eli beside me. Cam and Vel were summoned to the First-Born straight after events; Eli helped me to the bench while Luc snarled something in dragon tongue and walked away.

Eli's hot hands run across my forehead, and I wince at the twinge from the bruise. He smiles wryly. The bloody marks and growing bruises stand out on the Ivory Prince's pale skin, his plump lip split. But he ignored his own injures to tend to me, immediately helping me from the ground with firm hands and supporting me as we walked away. He must've seen the tears brimming in my eyes but said nothing.

"I can fix this for you. Gods, you make some stupid decisions, Ria."

Then Eli never saw or sensed the magic? "I can't help if I find Cam irresistible," I say, half-joking.

He smiles and winces as it pulls on his lip. "Hmm. That

move will cause him problems, since we all saw who instigated that kiss. I'm talking about the decision to attack Vel."

I swallow. It wasn't a decision. Not a fully conscious one.

"I fight back when I'm threatened," I say and rub my neck and something stings. Did Cam's talons cut me? "And I'm known to be impulsive and resourceful."

Eli's lips purse and he strokes the spot on my neck that tingles, oddly both soothing and arousing. "That's the problem." He focuses on touching other places, as if applying a balm.

"Why am I being treated like this, Eli?"

He lifts his eyes to mine. "Because dragons are assholes, including the queen?"

"This is abusive shit, Eli. You have to help me leave before Vel kills me or I kill him." I tighten my fingers around his. "Didn't you say you'd do what I ask?"

Chuckling, Eli moves to kneel on the ground in front of me. "That's not what I meant. Give me your arm."

Obediently, I hold out my bruised arm and blink in surprise when his touch fades the bluish marks. "You have odd magic for a dragon."

"We're not all vicious bastards."

"You looked fairly vicious fighting with Vel."

He shrugs. "That's self-defense. I don't hurt unless I'm provoked." His fingers stroke my forearm and I'm lulled by the sensation for a few moments.

"I can't bond with Vel," I say. "Please help me."

Eli takes my other arm to check for injuries. "My hands are tied Ria. If that's what's decided by the First-Born, I've no choice."

I gawk. "But they're practically imprisoning and forcing me to do this."

With a sigh, he places his hands on my knees instead. "We

won't stay in Reodian forever. If you're Vel's—" I pull a face "—and we go somewhere, you'll come. What you decide to do once you're outside of Reodian is your choice."

"Are you saying you'd let me go?"

He squeezes my knees. "I never said that. But I heard you're a mercenary's daughter who's adept at sneaking. Who knows? You might sneak away."

I slump back against the stone bench. "Do you all agree on that?"

He purses his lips. "On what, Aurelia?"

"Me..." I sigh. He won't say what he's alluding to, but I have to hope that I'm right. *Me escaping.* "Before anything else, I've a furious prince to deal with."

"Yes. Quite the humiliation." Eli shifts to sit beside me on the bench again. "Vel will behave himself in public."

"And in private?" I ask warily.

Eli lowers his voice. "One thing about Velanor—he's more mouth than action. Too hot headed to think things through."

"Doesn't that make him more dangerous?" I ask.

"In the moment, perhaps. But he's easy to outsmart before he does anything but lash out." Eli pulls fingers through my tangled hair. "How you behaved in the arena— that's too like *him*. We're all aware he's behaving like an asshole, and Vel knows we won't stand for mistreating a woman. So, be clever and let him fuck up."

"I hope you're right," I mumble. "I don't know why I'm put in this position, but I need to get out."

Eli's eyes go distant for a moment. "There's a lot happening here, Ria. I need you to be smart and figure things out because I can't tell you much."

My heart lurches. "What? Are you all hiding something?"

He scoffs to himself. "I don't think you're the only one with things hidden from you. For now, you're safe."

Somebody clears their throat nearby and I look up to see

the flame-haired guard who brought me here from Vel's court. "You are required to return to the court now, Aurelia," he says stiffly, then glances at Eli.

"Is Vel recovering?" he asks the guard.

"Recovering from what?"

Eli smiles. "Nothing. I shall see you tonight, Ria. Try to keep out of trouble before then." I swallow at the thought of being alone in that room where Vel can reach me. "And leave your rope behind when you accompany Vel to the gathering."

The guard looks between us, brow tugged down.

If only Eli's joke was funny.

CHAPTER 26

AURELIA

As I RELUCTANTLY RETURN TO MY CHAMBERS, THOUGHTS bounce around my mind.

The rising magic.

Cam's kiss.

How the fury at the position the dragons placed me in didn't ebb and drove me to an insane act. I could've run from the arena, but instead I wanted to *hurt* him. *Humiliate* the bastard.

Vel's weak. Not because I managed to half-strangle him, but because he'll follow orders to do something he detests— bond with me. And he's prepared to attack his friends to stay as the Talindra's favorite. Or is this an act? Is his real weakness the desire for power at any cost?

I'm confused, aching, and constantly questioning why I reacted in that way. Yes, I was scared and angry, but that move with the rope? Insane. When Cam first informed me about my Ebon 'origins' and my family confirmed this, I'd worried the magic would emerge uncontrolled from my body. I never thought this hidden Ebon would take hold of my *mind,* too.

And Cam's kiss—did he mean to surprise me in the way Devin's slap once did, or was there more? Something clashed with mine, that storm exploding the darkness, his power launched at mine.

Is the challenge Cam made only from one dragon to another over a female, the group treating me as an object to be batted around and played with again? Cam told Vel he wanted the role assigned to the winner. Whatever Cam's motivations, I'm no better off even if the First-Born *did* change their minds who I bonded to and handed me to Cam.

After one day in Reodian, my only goal is to leave.

I spend the rest of the afternoon on tenterhooks, expecting Vel to seek revenge on me privately, but the only person who enters my room is Mal, with a meal of chicken and potatoes that I struggle to eat. Mal doesn't ask questions nor talk to me in the candid way he did earlier. Does he know what happened because this must be the rite he mentioned?

Instead, he reminded me I'm to dress for a gathering and to make myself look decent as he appraised my disheveled state. He informed me there were fresh clothes in my wardrobe, and I requested hair pins and ribbons to 'pretty myself'.

If only he knew why

Returning shortly with the items, he again barely spoke and left.

He *does* know and is pissed that I've humiliated his friend.

Somebody left new clothing in the armoire, fortunately since the dress I wore earlier is torn and filthy. I'm stubborn, but not stubborn enough to walk into a royal gathering dressed in the worse for wear items I arrived in either. Not that I could because that same somebody removed them from the room while I was absent.

After years living life in the way I want, equal to any man, I'm struggling with the invasion. Why didn't my family tell me who I am? I could've prepared myself for this situation instead of finding myself thrown into this huge pile of shit. Surely, they didn't believe the dragons would never find me? Or had my family fooled themselves that whatever existed inside me *didn't*, since I'd shown no inclination to anybody but Devin?

Accepting my next fate, I wash away the dirt from earlier in the huge, circular tub of the bathing room beside my chamber and brush my hair out loose around my shoulders, impressed with the shine. How ladylike. Then, I set about winding the red ribbons inside a braid which I fumbled to pin around my head in the way Calla does for noble gatherings. This takes three frustrating attempts and when I'm done, I stare back at the elegant lady in the mirror.

At least Vel can't complain that I don't look the part.

I can't remember the last time I wore an elegant dress. Possibly an Aureate Court event? A choice of three now hang in front of me, all ruby red to match my dragon nemesis. With a sigh, I drag each one out and place them on the bed. All are long, and all a soft, silken material, but each cut differently in varying degrees of modesty. I'm not wearing the one with a stranglingly high neckline, nor the one with skirts split along each thigh and up to my ass, so choose the lesser of the three evils. The chosen dress's neckline dips lower than I'd like but only reveals the slightest curve of my breasts and the skirts touch my ankles. The silk appears different shades of red depending on where the light catches, and since the dress clings to my curves, if I still had a dagger, I'd struggle to conceal one beneath the tight fit.

Slipping my feet into soft shoes, I wait for release from the boredom, still fearful what will happen when Vel sees me.

The door swings open without anybody knocking, and I instinctively spring to my feet. Vel stands in the entry, and we silently stare at each other. I've met nobles and royalty dressed in finery too many times than I care to remember, but never one who dressed as ostentatiously as Vel. Elves often overdress, their garish colors hurting my eyes and the painted faces emphasizing their difference to humans. This dragon's long scarlet jacket is buttoned in gold, a trim around the edges, a gold shirt beneath.

Gold.

Never in my life have I seen clothing woven from gold. His black boots reach to his knees with buckles to match and his hair is pulled from his shimmering face, kohl around his eyes.

The amount of jewelry on his hands and around his neck adds to the excessive appearance, but would I expect any less?

"You should knock. I could've been half-naked," I retort.

"Yet you aren't." He firmly closes the door behind him, and my mouth goes totally dry. "I'm glad you've discarded the filthy clothes. You reeked."

"Charming."

The silence that follows is thick with the unsaid; I dart a look to the door, but he's too close to pass.

"Are you worried that I'll hurt you, Aurelia?" he asks quietly and steps forward.

My eyes go to his neck. If Vel were human, he'd have evidence of my attack on his skin, but his skin is unmarked.

Vel takes a long look at me, and hairs raise on my neck as his gaze lingers on my breasts and then my lips. "We need a truce of sorts, if we are to deal with..." He sucks his teeth. "The situation."

"Situation?" I say and swallow, still wary an assault may come at any moment. "What do we do?"

"I can't do anything." The shimmer on his face doesn't detract from the dark look. "But after this afternoon's *debacle*, the elders spoke to me and demanded we treat each other with respect in public."

Respect? We glower at each other.

"I'm prepared to do so if you acquiesce to me, Aurelia. And you must behave tonight. If you humiliate me in any way, I'll make things unpleasant for you." He closes the gap between us, and my blood pulses harder as he looms over me. "In private."

"Oh. I thought you might lure out the evil queen in front of everybody," I say.

A smile snakes across his face. "I'll choose my moment."

"Good luck, since I've no malice."

"Earlier wasn't malice?" He slants his head. "Did something *stir* in you, Aurelia?"

His red eyes gleam at me, and I hold his gaze. "Stirred inside me that caused me to kiss Cam?"

"A decision he'll regret." Vel reaches out and I freeze as his rough knuckles brush my cheek. "Challenging another flight's prince for his upcoming bonded is frowned on and could cause a rift between courts."

"But you don't want me. Nor do I want you." Where his hand touched burns as if he branded me.

"Regardless, I won't allow Cam to make me appear weak."

"Tonight. Do the other dragons know who I am?" I ask.

"All believe this is a political match to aid relations between dragons and humans. Personally, I'd like them to know the truth but this is Talindra's wish."

Like everything is Talindra's wish.

He pokes the tip of his tongue against a canine. "Here's the deal. We do as the elders ask, but then... nothing."

"Why not just help me leave?" I retort. "Neither of us want to fuck each other."

He blinks at my language. "Because the First-Born have plans that they need your help with."

"Such as?"

"Such as you help and *then* you can leave. I'm sure they'll discuss this with you soon."

I huff. "Why are you all deceiving me?"

"Everything we do is for the good of the realms—dragon, elf, and human."

He frowns as I scoff. "Vel. How can you accept your elders forcing you into this?"

Vel's voice lowers. "We only need to fuck once. You might even enjoy it."

"By the fire on the island, you informed me how violently you fuck, add to that your obvious hatred of me, and I very much doubt I would." I step away. "No. You don't touch me."

Arms behind his back, Vel steps forward and leans forward, and his breath ruffles my hair. "As with everything else in this situation, you have no choice. And neither do I."

"You *do*!" I protest.

He arches a brow. Our challenge continues and I'm aware what must happen. Contrary to my normal behavior, I'll need to avoid any conflict with a man who belittles and insults me. I'll give him no reason to speak to or taunt me.

Eli mentioned that we'd leave at some point, even hinted he'd turn his back if I ran. I'm praying there's either a route from the court where it's possible to pass into human lands, or a way from Reodian that doesn't involve flight. Then I'll leave. I don't care if I spend my whole life in exile. I'm accustomed to living by my wits; I'll survive.

Once I escape.

CHAPTER 27

AURELIA

The moment my soft-soled feet step into the ballroom at Reodian's central palace, I scan the gathered dragons for the other princes. I'd like to speak to Cam about earlier, not only the kiss and his decision to challenge Vel, but if he disclosed to anybody else about the shadow that stirred in me.

I'd partly forgotten that they won't stand out due to their hair color as they did in the inn, since every dragon here has their flight's appearance. Oddly, most are male, many dressed as ostentatiously as Vel as if the number of jeweled rings or detail of the embroidery on their tunics denotes status. Yet they can't hide the inhuman edge to their elegance, not only the powerful bodies with muscles rarely seen on men, but the way they hold themselves. These dragons exude an intangible primal energy—one that scares some humans and elves but captivates others.

The ones I glance at don't have horns; this appears to only

be a First-Born trait. The few female dragons attending stand close to the men's sides and keep their eyes lowered. I frown to myself. The position of women in this society bothers me —especially considering the realm is practically governed by one. Like Talindra, they're an impressive height and are closer to the female elven form than a human one, more muscular and less curves. Not that there's anything masculine in the pretty gowns and bejeweled hair.

A dragon's gathering matches any elven or human one that I've reluctantly attended in the past, only the music is different, played on stringed instruments resembling harps, the high ceiling creating a softer acoustic. Nobody dances, they merely walk from person to person, shouting and laughing in a decidedly un-noble way. In the center of the room, a fountain dribbles across a silver sphere and my mouth drops open as I watch dragons scoop goblets through the water in a small trough, drinking the contents that drip down their hands, or passing to others.

All the flights are represented, and dozens in attendance makes my search for the other princes more difficult. I huff, already perspiring in the crowded room squinting as the wide glass chandeliers and lights on the wall intensify the golds and silvers trimming the walls. Naturally, focus homes in on me and I flash smiles at those who stare too long. The whispering annoys me, and I catch the word 'Ebon' several times. At least Vel didn't insist I wear black.

Mal accompanies us, not the only guard in the room, although he appears assigned to me because he's at my side as I follow Vel.

"Are you my bodyguard or jailor?" I ask him as he falls into step beside me.

"A little of both."

"Should I be worried that someone might harm me?" My

eyes dart around at the sheer number of people who dwarf me, many looking at me in disdain.

"Unlikely, but as a prince Vel likes to ensure he always has a guard with him."

"Another would harm the prince?" I halt.

Mal's eyes fill with mirth. "You may be surprised to hear this, but Vel often upsets people."

We exchange wry smiles, and Vel throws a look at us from over his shoulder. He jerks his head at those scrutinizing our behavior; gritting my teeth, I scurry to catch up.

"Mal, please attend to Aurelia's needs until the First-Born arrive. I have other matters." He flicks his tongue against his top teeth and the slow appraisal of me from head to toe tightens my belly. "And ensure she stays away from the other princes."

"Why?" I retort. "At least they're friendly."

Vel lowers his voice, and my heart rate spikes as his large palm rests in the small of my back, drawing me closer. Nearby, somebody murmurs. "Because you unfortunately belong to me, and I don't want anybody questioning my control over you."

His hand slides away, and I watch him walk away, cheeks firing. Belong to him? I don't fucking think so. Vel just *strengthened* my desire to find the others.

His words echo. *Do not humiliate me.*

I side-glance Mal, who stares ahead, expressionless. "I'll find you a drink. Take care with dragon wine."

"I've drunk some before," I reply as he leads me to the fountain.

The fizzy wine tastes better than that from the cabin, smoother and sweeter. Mal continues to guide me around the room like a sheepdog would a dumb ewe, sharply moving me away every time somebody approaches.

"Am I banned from speaking to people?" Not that I want to.

"Vel would rather you didn't."

I swear beneath my breath. *You are the one who can control her.* We reach an alcove where the ruby crest looks down on us, a wrought silver lantern beneath. Mal rests against the wall beside me and drinks his wine.

"You don't behave like someone with a lesser standing than these people," I comment.

"I'm Vel's chief guard. I've more sway."

"Yet you're tasked with sitting outside my chamber all night?" I drink too. "Surely that's a duty for a less senior guard."

"Vel doesn't trust anybody else." The steady gaze flushes my cheeks. Am I seeing intent in his eyes too?

"This bond," I say. "Cam once said the idea is old-fashioned and not a true bonding. Is that right?"

"To the younger dragons, yes, but Vel's a prince and therefore follows tradition insisted on by the First-Born." Mal scratches the corner of his eye. "He can't touch anybody else once you're bonded, although..."

"Although what?" I ask as his lips purse.

"You don't want to fuck him, so that bond might be an issue."

The wine spurts from my mouth, showering his leather jerkin. "Vel said we have no choice. That's why I need to leave."

"Mmm. As I said, an issue." He shrugs. "The First-Born will sense whether you're bonded or not. There's no choice. Unless." Mal turns his gaze to mine. "You fuck another dragon first."

My jaw drops open. "Are you propositioning me?"

His loud bark of a laugh draws attention. "No. Vel would

kill me, no questions asked." *Another dragon.* "Another prince?" I whisper.

Cam's kiss. His claim.

Mal gives me a long look before returning his scrutiny to the crowds. Through the crowds, I spot where Vel stands, and although I can't see him clearly, it's obviously him from the number surrounding. "If you want to take a risk—and the other prince does too. Vel and the First-Borns' reaction can't be predicted."

"The others don't want to bond either." I sigh.

"Oh, they wouldn't pay attention to that tradition."

Something doesn't add up here. This man is supposedly Vel's right-hand and most trusted guard, yet he's telling me how to evade this bond and marriage. "What's the deal, Malanor?"

"Deal?" His eyes return to mine.

"Vel told you to keep me away from the other princes yet you're practically telling me to seduce one." I narrow my eyes. "You have a motive."

"Perhaps I don't like to see you forced into something against your will." He smiles. "I know that you might try to fight your way out of this situation, but I advise you to take care and be more creative."

But his suggestion has merit.

I stand under his watch for an inordinately boring length of time, constantly searching amongst those gathered for the other princes. Have they washed their hands of me now the challenge is over? Cam promised he'd keep me safe but has Talindra's decree overrode that possibility?

I slump against the alcove wall and drain my glass before holding it out to Mal. "More wine. Please."

Expecting him to say no, I'm surprised when he wanders away to the central flowing fountain of wine leaving a warning not to move. The moment his head disappears amongst a group, Cam emerges from one nearby. I should've spotted him earlier, the sapphires stitched into the lapels of his well-cut jacket, the deep blue shirt beneath stretching across his chest, and the way he seems to *shine* more, as Vel does.

I peer behind, expecting to see the others. Cam glances around and walks towards me, so I open my mouth to speak but he walks by. For a heartbeat, I'm pissed at his ignoring me until a large hand surrounds mine and he drags me after him, silently.

CHAPTER 28

AURELIA

I ATTEMPT NOT TO TRIP OVER MY FEET AS CAM TAKES LONG strides through the crowd and through a door leading into a quiet hallway.

"What's happening?" I ask as he continues to pull me along. To the left, arched windows look out over a courtyard I passed through earlier. Where are we going?

"Cam. Tell me what—"

"Fuck."

I'm spun around, back to the wall, his whole body obscuring me from view. He presses himself against me as he did in the arena but this time I couldn't move if I tried. The power in these dragons' body is beyond anything I've encountered. My breath catches as he gazes down at me and I'm about to talk when I hear two voices moving closer.

"Guards." Cam's closer still, my head almost pressed to his lower chest.

I nod, the footsteps growing closer, and then my eyes widen as a large palm cups my ass.

A male chuckles. "I thought the Emerald Prince was the one for public fucking."

Gods. I tense, expecting the guards to pause but they continue. Cam watches them go, not moving an inch and I'm smothered against seeing anything.

"You can get your hand off of my ass now," I hiss at him. "And tell me what's happening."

"We need to talk." He steps back and looks from side to side. "Mal will look for you. Come quickly."

I only have a moment to catch the dark consternation on Cam's face before I trip after him as he pulls me away. Ahead, Luc stands side-on and speaks to the two guards.

My stomach lurches. Distracting them?

Reaching out to a door on our left, Cam pushes down the handle and leads me inside. I blink at the shadowy surroundings after the glaring light in the hallway. Cam moves to the window, making himself visible thanks to the moonlight. A few seconds later, Eli slips through the door too.

Everything tightens because neither look happy, dark consternation on Cam's face.

"We don't have much time. Listen," says Cam as Eli stands close to the door, back to us.

On guard.

"Time to do what?" I ask. "Are you planning to continue this challenge against Vel?"

He snorts. "No. The First-Born's plans aren't as innocent as they make out." My eyes widen. "Your life isn't in danger—yet—but you need to take care. Don't let anybody provoke you again. Look how easily your fear triggered something."

"I know that," I say, bewildered. "I've already decided not to engage with Vel."

"I don't think that'll work." Eli looks over his shoulder before returning his watch to the door.

Cam rubs fingers cross his lips. "The First-Born want your Ebon shadow," Cam explains. "If you allow yourself to relinquish control over that, you'll never leave the dragon realms."

"Because they'll kill me?" I ask, the wine in my stomach churning.

"Cam." Eli's voice comes in warning.

"Already?" he groans.

"Yes."

"Already what?" I ask, increasingly bewildered.

"I'll try to head him off." Eli quietly opens the door and slides through before it clicks softly behind him.

"Mal will detect you're with me." Cam runs a hand through his hair. "Listen. Vel plans to assault you. Frighten you."

A trembling starts in my hands and runs through every part of me. "What do you mean 'assault'?"

"If he brings out some of your shadow, he'll please the elders. Don't let him scare you. Call his bluff because I know he won't follow through. Vel will ensure you *think* he will, but even he wouldn't stoop that low."

"Follow through *what*?" But my skin crawls with fear. What Vel hinted earlier—that I'd have no choice but to fuck him. "No. Vel wanted a witness to my Ebon power."

"And he'll have one," says Cam. "Mal stands outside your door."

"Vel knows I can protect myself," I say.

"Without a dagger you'll only have one way. The magic."

"I don't have magic," I protest.

Cam sighs and takes both hands in his, mine clammy against his hot palms. "I know you do, because I interrupted that before when I kissed you."

201

A breath escapes at the memory, at how each time Cam kisses me I'm filled with a desire I don't understand, one that radiates towards me now. "Are you in a lot of trouble for that challenge? Vel said you were."

Cam shakes his head. "I'll deal with that. Just remember what I'm telling you and keep calm." He cups my cheek. "I promise that if Vel does hurt you, I'll rip his cock off. If I see one bruise on you tomorrow, he'll fucking regret it."

Air is slugged from my lungs. "He plans to *rape* me?"

"Threaten." My breathing becomes short pants. "Ria, he doesn't want the bond so why would he force himself on you? But you also know how violent and frightening he can be— he'll tell you that he's changed his mind and that you have to comply."

I'm dumbfounded, unable to speak, bile rising to my throat. Cam holds my cheeks and tips my face upward. "Call his bluff. Don't listen to the shadow inside."

The floor lurches beneath my feet and I allow myself a memory I've denied for two years. "This happened once before," I croak. "I won't cope."

"What? Somebody touched you without consent?" snarls Cam. "Who?"

"Two men from Devin's guild." I moisten my lips. "I don't remember much but something frightened them, and they tried to run."

"Two men?" Cam's voice becomes a snarl. "I want their names."

"What?" I shake my head. "My father is an assassin, Cam. They're dead."

His nostrils flare. "Vel won't let any of us into his court right now so I can't help but please, please keep control. *Take control*. There's nothing he'll hate more. If Vel thinks you've changed your mind and *want* to fuck him, his plan to provoke your Ebon becomes pointless."

"Oh, gods." I clutch Cam's sleeve. "Can't you take me with you to *your* court?"

"Not yet. Ria, I'm sorry. I'll try to speak to you about this more but if the elders discover..." His fingers dig into my cheeks. "I feel bound to my promise to Luin and by your connection to my flight. I wish I'd known. *I* would've bonded with you."

I blink at him. "That's crazy."

He gives a half-smile. "Did you not hear what Calla said about *why* she and Luin are bonded? I was half-serious in my challenge earlier."

"Luin and Calla bonded to protect her from the First-Born but that won't work with me."

"No, but it would keep you out of Vel's hands."

Hands. I swallow the hard lump in my throat. "I hope this isn't an elaborate ploy to get me to fuck you, Cam."

He makes a derisive noise at my half-joke. "Much as I'd enjoy that, if the First-Born find my scent all over you, I'm in a lot of trouble."

"Isn't it already?" I ask. "You pinned me to the wall."

"Not that type of scent." He sighs and smooths a strand of hair that escaped my braid. "You look so different to that assassin I seduced."

I scowl. "You didn't seduce me."

"You *planned* to take me to bed?" His mouth tips into a smile as fingers touch my mouth. "Do you know how close I came to not stopping unless you told me to?"

Cam's fingertips are coarse against my lips, the sensation tingling across my face. "If I had, would we be bonded?" I ask hoarsely.

"Only if the First-Born knew but by the time we returned your scent on me would've long faded." He trails a soft line along my cheek. "But those minutes in that room have a grip on me now. I don't know if this is the Ebon or more."

203

I swallow at his mentioning the Ebon. "You have to help me, Cam. Take me from here."

He rests his forehead against mine, and I'm barely aware as he draws me closer. "You're asking me to give up everything. To leave my duties. I can't."

"Then I'll find my way out alone," I say.

A hand tightens in the small of my back and our bodies are flush as he presses a kiss to my forehead. "Deal with one thing at a time. Vel is your problem tonight."

"Maybe *he'll* help," I mumble. "Vel doesn't want me here."

Cam tips my chin with his thumb and forefinger. "You're his key to power."

But I want Cam. He's looking at me with affection and concern, not the disdain that surrounds me so much. This man cares. I tangle my fingers into his long hair and press my mouth to his, urging him into a kiss. He takes no persuading as he grabs my ass, holding me against him, as his tongue eagerly meets mine.

Ever since the first kiss, I've yearned for Cam, the moment creating a connection our bodies want. Was the bond created without a physical union? Cam pulls me forward as he backs up against the wall, his kiss growing more demanding, cock hardening against my belly. As my hands sneak between us, trying to push beneath his shirt, there's a low growl in his throat.

Cam catches my wrist and pulls his mouth away. "Ria. I'm not fucking you here."

"I wasn't going to," I say hoarsely.

"Do you think we're in control of this? Because I don't." He takes a ragged breath. "As soon as I taste you, I lose my mind. I'm holding on to the part who wants to take his time and not fuck you in a darkened room where I can't see you."

"Then let me come with you tonight," I whisper.

"Ria." He rests his forehead on mine. "Do you want me to

piss off the First-Born more than I did earlier? Talindra is obsessive about bonding you with Vel. She might remove me altogether."

"I fucking hate her," I blurt.

Cam places soft kisses on my cheeks, presses his lips to my closed eyelids and then forehead. "Stay strong. I've spoken to Eli and Luc. Somehow, we'll get you out. I promise."

The door behind slams against a wall as someone throws it open. "What the fuck are you doing with Aurelia?" comes Mal's furious voice.

Crap.

"I'm following your advice," I say nonchalantly and turn around. "Unfortunately, Cam said no, so I suppose I'll try one of the others."

Mal's stony expression remains as he slams the door behind and sizes up the scene. "Cam?"

"What can I say? She's a seductress." He gives Mal a tight smile. "I discovered that when she tried to fuck me the first night we met."

"Aurelia. Get back to the gathering," Mal says icily. "And I can't believe you were so stupid, Cam."

"When I do, I won't be quick," Cam whispers then moves me firmly away from him by the shoulders. "Such a wicked girl."

With a wink, he saunters by, pausing as he looks at Mal. "I suggest you don't mention this to Velanor. Because if he knows Ria tried to fuck me, there'll be trouble—for *you* because I'll know who informed him."

I make to follow Cam, but Mal moves to block my way. "I was joking when I told you to fuck a different prince."

"Are you sure?" I arch a brow.

"Do you think I'd be so disloyal?"

"How loyal are you to him?" I ask. "Are you happy that he's planning to break me until my Ebon fights back?"

Mal's expression shutters. "I can offer you advice. Ria, this is who you are. Perhaps see your time here as an opportunity to embrace what you are and decide how to use that dragon inside."

I narrow my eyes at him. "I'm not a dragon, Malanor."

"Your mother contained a tiny part of a dragon soul, Ria. You know this. She also lay with a dragon in the time she carried you in her body. The Ebon Queen died, and Calla took on her essence in the very early days, before she knew she was with child." For a moment I think he's about to touch me, but he crosses his arms instead. "Calla's human body wasn't enough, but there's enough dragon within *your* body for the Ebon soul to plant into yours and grip tight."

"No," I say hoarsely. "I'm not a dragon. I don't shift. I was fathered by a human."

"Don't underestimate what you are and what you can do." He reaches behind himself to open the door. "I don't need to help you because you have the power to help yourself."

CHAPTER 29

AURELIA

I worried about Vel's response after earlier today, but in comparison I'm panic-stricken when Talindra approaches me through the crowd, everybody watching who she makes a beeline to. Me. My mouth goes completely dry, contrasting how damp my palms become.

Talindra stops, close enough for me to see how her eyes match Vel's and at how smooth her skin, as if her lips and eyes are painted on stone. I try hard not to gawk at the small horns protruding from beneath her red hair, which is difficult because tonight they're decorated by loose gold chains, similar to what female dragons around us have on their ears.

I can't comprehend what her anger would be like considering everything else about the Ruby First-Born is magnified compared to Vel.

Including her teeth which are *all* sharp, revealed when she smiles.

"Aurelia," she says in her lilting tone, face nothing but open friendliness. "I do hope you forgive us for subjecting you to our little ritual."

She thinks *that's* the worst thing she inflicted on me? "I'm unhappy about the situation, Talindra. I want to leave."

"Political marriages can be tricky."

"Excuse me?" I breathe out. "I'm not royalty nor would my father allow such a situation."

The mask of friendliness flickers for a moment. "Yet here we are." I fight recoiling when her soft hands take mine in both of hers. "We need to control the Ebon. A promise to the human king is a promise I must keep. We can guide you, Aurelia."

Around, the voices and music fade away until only blood pulses in my ears. Cam and Mal both spoke of things I struggle to understand. *Is* my future inevitable? "Guide me how?"

Talindra's hands remain in mine. "Female dragons are powerful, Aurelia. Our influence is greater. I saw hints of that within you today. Velanor is your perfect match, and you shall realize this in time."

"Yet you have three consorts; why should I have one?"

I immediately regret the words as her red eyes flare brighter. "Because I am the First-Born, Aurelia."

Did Lyrandra's death suit Talindra in some way beyond destroying evil? These dragons speak of the Ebon flight as ambitious and ruthless; a leader who went too far, but are the Ruby flight any different? Talindra's chokehold on the hierarchy is clear.

A sudden shiver runs through.

Is she pairing the Ebon with the Ruby for a reason nobody is aware of? She seemed pleased *and* unsurprised when Vel won their challenge. Mal's words about the dragon within... if that's true our union could create something more.

"Aurelia?" Talindra squeezes my fingers. "Are you alright?"

I force a smile. "Like I said, I'm finding the situation *difficult*."

Again, she ignores my pointed response. "Come. Let me introduce you. You look delightful, by the way. Such a beauty."

Talindra leads me through those gathered who're pretending not to study the human brought into their midst —one that their aloof queen holds by the hand as she walks through them.

As we reach the other First-Born, I watch as the three all approach and kiss Talindra, one by one, before standing at her side like obedient guards.

Talindra's influence over these men solidifies her position as the true leader of all flights.

Their obvious devotion aids her power.

The way to change my fate crystallizes—I can't ever escape the dragons, so I need to follow Mal's advice. Embrace what I am.

Become a dragon queen.

Become Talindra.

The dragon princes must become *my* consorts.

Vel steps forward, expression blank as he holds out a hand, a prince welcoming his bonded match. I smile warmly at him as he draws me to stand beside him, then Vel tenses in surprise as I tiptoe to place my lips on his.

When some dragons close by clap gently, murmurings rippling through, I lace my fingers through Vel's before turning to the smiling subjects.

"What the fuck are you doing?" he asks quietly.

"Accepting my new future. I hope you do too."

All of them must become mine. But holding his hand turns my stomach after what Cam told me. This man— creature—has no pity for how his behavior would affect me.

He'd happily place a woman in a position where she's terrified of an assault. Do I want him as a consort? This dragon would never bow to me or turn against his queen. Perhaps I'd need to deal with him in other ways.

I'm barely aware of the introductions from Talindra, only catching briefly how our wedding and bonding will take place 'imminently' whatever the fuck that means. A couple of times, I glance at Vel whose acting skills are perfect as he manages to look *proud*.

Ugh.

I'm hopeful that once this scrutiny ends, I can retreat back to a corner with my bodyguard, while Vel continues the political moves with the dragons who target him.

No such luck.

I have to dance with my betrothed.

Under inspection by everybody, a smiling Vel takes my hand and leads me to the dance floor. We stand face to face, and I hesitate. In an official, respectful dance pose, Vel holds one of my arms and winds his other around my waist. People part to give us space, and Vel doesn't speak, holding my eyes with his. I catch the dragon's scent; a subtle warmth to the cologne underpinned by an aura they all have. One that does unwanted things to me.

If I kissed the others in the way I kissed Cam, would the same unspoken, uncontrollable bond happen? Even Velanor?

"This is a little different to last time we touched," I say as we step around the floor.

His answer is a growl.

"What has Talindra said to you?" I ask. "I expected you to retaliate against me."

Our gazes remains locked. "To follow protocol and not trigger whisperings from other dragons that Talindra made a mistake in pairing us."

"How can you let her force you?" I whisper.

Vel pulls me closer until my bare skin brushes his tunic's stiff material; not close enough to touch the heat and muscle beneath but enough to fire an unwanted desire. "The same way I'll force *you*."

His words snuff that fire out and I look away.

Vel's grip around my waist tightens, and I focus on maintaining our rhythm. My mother desperately tried to teach me to dance as a child in order to take part in court gatherings but that was years ago. The only dancing that I partake in these days is drunkenly in inns, so I need to focus hard on not tripping over Vel's feet.

"I saw you walk from this room with Cam." Vel's breath strokes my cheek as he says the words. "If rumors spread about the pair of you, there'll be consequences. And if anybody discovers what he did in the arena? Well... Not good."

"I like him. He's an honorable man. Dragon," I say, not moving my cheek. "He's Sapphire flight and I have a connection to them."

"No dragon is honorable with a human, Aurelia," he says, breath again ruffling my hair—and me.

Vel was raised a prince, but he emanates something that he'd possess without that station. His killer body and sculpted features are accompanied by the self-assurance that crosses the line to arrogance. He'd have any woman in his thrall—I saw that when watching him as I stood with Mal earlier.

Despite my misgivings, I hope I can do the same to him. I've no real plans *how* I'll convince the other princes to join me, especially if they see this could affect Talindra. But if my essence attracts them, that's half the battle.

Vel may take some convincing but even he'll have a weak spot.

I resist relaxing into the dance and allowing any closer

contact with Vel, my silence already handing him a victory. As if aware, Vel's hold on me becomes firmer, possessive, which doesn't help the images floating into my mind—his mouth seeking mine, large hands running fingers across my skin.

See? The attraction of our essences will aid me.

"How many dances must we have?" I mutter.

Vel pulls his head back and regards me silently, as we weave around the people, trapped in a dance of our own, oblivious to anything but each other and what underpins us. "We only need to perform once."

His facial expression tells me to pay heed to the undertones, and I know exactly what this means. Is he beginning his threats now to unnerve me, so that I'm already worried when he approaches my room?

The music stops and a nearby couple bump us. Vel and I stand face to face as I break contact with him, fighting a relieved sigh.

"Duty done?" I ask him.

He looks over my shoulder. "Mal. Watch her. No speaking to others, Aurelia."

I make a scornful noise. "Trying to control my life already, husband?"

Shock at the word flickers across his face before the disdain returns. "And especially don't speak to Camanor or the other flight princes."

"I understand. You want me all to yourself." I give a coy smile, loving his confusion and annoyance.

Aware of eyes upon us again, I stroke Vel's cheek before brushing my lips on his once more. This time he doesn't withdraw but holds the back of my head before I can. "Don't start what you can't finish, Aurelia," he murmurs.

I step away. "Thank you for the dance, Vel."

A dance that'll continue until one of us outmaneuvers the other.

Talindra looks between us, head slanted as Vel walks away and she tips her chin as our eyes meet.

Velanor isn't the only Ruby dragon I need to outmaneuver.

CHAPTER 30

AURELIA

THANKS TO CAM, I'M PREPARED FOR VEL.

When will the dumb dragon accept that my upbringing means I don't need a dagger to fight efficiently? Didn't he experience that today?

Vel didn't approach me again following the dance, and I kept away from the other princes, more due to the First-Borns' presence than his instructions. Of course, the women at the occasion targeted the princes, and I watched, thin-lipped, as they laughed and flirted with each other, a spike of disgust hitting my heart when I saw Cam's hands on somebody else.

Will I have to fight through other females to reach and seduce the princes?

Seduce. Ha. These men won't need any seducing, apart from *one* who'll be a challenge. The one who's about to learn not to toy with me.

I'm unsure if Mal is still stationed outside my room so I'm

not positive that the footsteps are Vel's until the door opens without him knocking. He doesn't see me at first as I recline on an armchair with my feet on the low table, ankles crossed but still wearing the dress, hair still pinned.

"What a pleasant surprise," I say.

He jerks his head as he notices me. "Wrong."

I stand and approach before placing a hand on his muscular chest. "I enjoyed our dance earlier."

If it weren't for the sheer distaste in his eyes, I'd appreciate how damn sexy this man is. I run my fingers across the top of his smooth skin where he's unbuttoned his shirt, and he crushes my wrist. I refuse to wince at the pain.

"What are you doing?" he snaps.

"Well, there's only one reason you'd visit my chamber at this time." I slowly moisten my lips enjoying the confusion clouding his expression. "And after our conversation earlier..."

"You think I'm here to fuck you?" He arches a brow. "Is that what you *want*?"

I step back from him and smooth his shirt. "As with you, I'm not keen on upsetting the elders. You said only once? Let's get this done with." His face remains tight, but his eyes betray his continued confusion. "Do you want to undress me, or should I?"

I can practically see his plans sliding away. *Asshole.*

Vel's hand circles my throat and he roughly pulls me forward. Glowing eyes look down into mine. "Are you playing games with me, Ebon?"

"You're not frightening me," I whisper. "Try harder."

"That's not a sensible thing to say."

"Mmm." Our gazes remain locked as I fight showing any nerves at how breakable my neck is. "I know that you want me. I felt how much when I rolled onto you at the inn."

Vel's nostrils flare and I pray that my plan works, and that he leaves "What can I say? The thought of hurting you aroused me."

Gods. "Luckily, I like a rough fuck."

Vel spins me around, hand now around the back of my neck as he shoves me against the wall. Face first. Hard. "Liar. I recall you said you *didn't*."

His body presses against me, including his stiffening cock. I bet *that* reaction makes him pissed. But fuck, what if he's telling the truth because that shallower breathing could be more than anger?

"Why don't we find out?" I reply, cheek squashed to the wall. "And if we're only going to do this once for the bond, make it good, Vel."

With a snarl, he spins me around, fingers digging into my shoulders as he looks down at me. "Don't provoke me, Aurelia."

Cam's body against mine earlier stirred a lust for him, his warmth and concern pushing me across the line to wanting him. With Vel, the mingling apprehension and anger fires something different—a desire to fight back and conquer him. I don't need Ebon dragon essence to do that.

Slipping my fingers into his trousers waistband, I yank Vel forward so our bodies are flush. "Devin interrupted my time with Cam. Ever since then, I've wanted to try out a dragon. I'd prefer Cam, but the bond..." My hand slides between us and air hisses between his teeth as my palm presses against his hard length.

"What the fuck are you doing, Aurelia?" His voice weakens as I refuse to.

"Did you come here thinking you could force me? Fight you as you assaulted me?" His cock is now rock hard against my hand and his expression doesn't change. "Is that what you like? I can pretend if you want?"

A primal noise rumbles in Vel's chest as he pulls me from

the wall and slaps my hand away from him, shoving me hard to one side until I stumble. "Come on, Vel. Show me what you can do. How does a dragon prince fuck?"

He's dumbfounded, breathing heavily as his plan disintegrates around his feet, and I drop my eyes to the size of him pressing against his pants.

The asshole put himself in a position that he never expected. He planned to frighten me—threaten me with something abhorrent. Now he's out of his depth and responding exactly how he doesn't want to.

He's turned on by my response, and I'll bring him to his fucking knees.

Closing the gap between us, I smack both hands into his chest, but he's immovable. "Come on, Vel. Fuck me. That's why you came." No response. "Velanor?"

Any moment now he's going to leave this room, dragon tail between his legs. *You'll need a better plan, Vel.* I mimic his earlier move and reach out to circle fingers around his throat, squeezing. Our gazes lock and however hard Vel tries to hide what I'm arousing in him, the connection we already have is clear.

Dragon to dragon, he wants the woman he hates. "Come on, Vel. Fuck me," I whisper and squeeze his neck tighter.

With a guttural sound, Vel wrenches my hand from his neck and catches my dress at the shoulders, pulling downward until the dress rips at the seams, exposing my breasts. He flicks a gaze at me then bunches the material in his hand, tearing further. The torn dress pools at my feet leaving me naked apart from undergarments. Eyes blazing, Vel's gaze remains trained on mine.

Fuck. Fuck. *Fuck.* "I guess the answer is *you* wanted to remove my clothes." I say lightly.

"Do you understand how much you'll regret provoking me?" he snarls as he clenches his fists by his sides.

I stroke Vel's face before I rest a palm on his cheek, tiptoeing until my mouth touches his, the other hand sliding between us again. "Yet, you're not doing anything bad to me."

Again, our gazes lock, the challenge silent but our need shared. I want him to leave defeated, but as he barely restrains himself, molten heat runs through at the thought of conquering this dragon. If his dragon senses don't register my arousal, I'll be surprised. I've fucked men after fighting with them before and angry sex can be fun, but this is another level.

How long can he hold back? I skim my tongue against his lips, and he groans softly, fingers now digging into my shoulders. One thing I do know is that a dragon can't harm his bonded and if I'm seen with injuries, the First-Born won't be happy.

"Your self-control is impressive," I murmur. "Considering how hard your cock is right now. Are you going to use it or not?"

Vel crushes my face between his hands, mouth sealing over mine as he forces his tongue into my mouth. I welcome him, fisting his hair as our tongues sweep together, teeth clashing. A growl rumbles in his chest and he shoves me backwards until I'm sprawled on the bed, his kiss and hands bruising and invading, possessing. The weight of him should frighten me but I maintain my fake nonchalance and manage to get a hand between us and fingers onto his pant's button. Vel shoves apart my legs with his knee and I whimper as he presses it against the aching part of me.

As Vel breaks the kiss and looks down, face a mask of lust, I keep mine neutral, working on freeing his cock. "How far are you prepared to go to think you've beaten me?" he snarls.

Biting my lip, I pull his cock from his pants and close my hand around his wide shaft, stroking along the length, before running a finger across a bead of moisture at the tip.

Fuck, he's big. "How far are you prepared to go to think *you've* won?"

His hand dives between my legs, tearing through my undergarments as his fingers reach my slick pussy. "Don't play games with me, Aurelia, because you won't like how I play."

"Dirty?" I whisper.

"By my rules." I gasp out as he roughly pushes a finger inside. Then another. My eyes flutter closed, as he begins to fuck me hard with them, stretching me as my arousal covers his fingers.

The noises he makes border on animalistic, the force he uses almost painful, and I fight crying out as more fingers push into me. As I work him too, I'm shocked how readily I'd let him replace his fingers with his cock, the challenge between us now disintegrating into us both taking what we want.

Mouth parted and eyes half closed, he watches as my breath speeds, his own quickening as I press my hand harder around him. He groans at me as I massage his balls, gripping him harder, and I smile at how badly he's lost this game.

"You like this?" I murmur. "Is this how tight you grip yourself?" His forehead rests on mine, panting. "Imagine how tight I'd be around you. How well I'd take your hard cock, Vel. Every. Single. Inch. As you fuck me hard until I'm begging you to stop."

A suppressed sound comes from Vel's throat, and my eyes widen as something warm covers my hand and exposed belly.

What the fuck? His hand stills, and he swears, pulling fingers from me and hauling himself up. I'm dazed as I watch him push his cock back into his pants, frowning at the damp patch on my skin. Vel refuses to meet my eyes before he turns away.

Oh.

Well.

That I never expected. Looks like Vel's poor self-control spreads to more than his temper.

I force myself to laugh at him, knowing full well I'll make the situation worse. "Don't start what you can't finish, Vel," I say, echoing his earlier words. "Or does this happen a lot?" He freezes with a hand on the doorknob. "Do you often walk away leaving your women unsatisfied?"

Vel spins around and strides back over, ruby eyes flaring with fury. My taunting has gone too far; I shrink back and prepare for an assault as he looms over me. Firm hands grip my thighs, and Vel yanks me to the edge of the bed, dropping to his knees. I kick out at him, bewildered, and Vel catches my ankle. I'm pulled further forward as he hooks that leg over a shoulder.

The bewilderment grows when he lowers his head, and that shifts to shocked surprise as he swipes his tongue the length of me before sucking on my clit. Involuntarily, I gasp out and buck against him, and his laughter sends more thrills through.

I'm held firm to the bed by a massive hand on my belly, his mouth and tongue relentless. I grasp onto his long hair, and writhe against his face as his fingers push back inside, pressing on a spot that almost undoes me completely.

I begin to murmur as the pressure builds, grinding harder against his face as he teases me higher. I've never had a man go down on me so expertly, so focused, or send me towards losing control this quickly. The orgasm takes hold suddenly and I cry out, moving against him as he holds me firm and continues to pleasure me as my muscles clench around his fingers. Vel's tongue doesn't relent, until I'm pushing at his head, unable to take any more.

"Vel," I pant out. "You've proved your point."

His mouth and hands leave me as he kneels up and then

over me, caging me with his arms, hands on the bed either side of my head.

Vel's face glistens. "I *never* leave a woman unsatisfied," he growls. There's no possibility I can feign disinterest now or ever again and I struggle to even my breathing as he looks down on me. "But I was fucking tempted to stop *just* before you came and leave you."

My body shakes with the pleasure still rushing through me, completely at his mercy right now. I choke a shocked sound as his hand holds my throat again, bared teeth close to my face.

"If you tell anybody about *any* of this, next time I'll make you scream and not for the right reasons." He squeezes my neck in a final warning and hauls himself to his feet, gaze roaming over my naked body. "So fragile, Aurelia."

Leaving behind the veiled threat, Vel walks from the room.

CHAPTER 31

CAMANOR

Only we use this room at the back of the cantina, our private space that everybody wants an invite to. Chaises are arranged around the windowless room, plump cushions on the floor, and always plenty of wine. A red gauze curtain marks the entrance from the cantina, but nobody dare enter if they're not asked.

If they're female, we won't say no, and the girl will know exactly what she's stepping into if she walks into our room. The princes' activities aren't a secret, but few speak about our nights. If they do, they won't be invited again. For some reason, fucking princes is the greatest source of some girls' pleasure, so their mouths stay shut.

Tonight, we brought back girls from the gathering rather than those who seek us out in the cantina. High-class dragons' daughters, no doubt one or two hoping that they'll catch themselves a prince. If Velanor's chosen a mate, we might too, and they want a chance.

If only they knew the truth.

Daughters like Kay from the Sapphire flight who insists on sitting in my lap and rubbing her ass against me. Sighing at her obviousness, I rest my head on the back of the chaise and stare at the ceiling. If I look around the room instead, I'll see which prince is fucking the girl making fake noises of enjoyment and I don't want to.

All I can think about is Ria's mouth on mine and as Kay coyly strokes her fingers along my leg, I'm half-tempted to shove the girl's head south so I can imagine Ria's the one sucking my cock. She's already trying to unbutton my pants. I tip the cup of wine down my throat then swat the girl's busy fingers away, glancing around for more wine.

Eli sits in the chair opposite, a girl kneeling at his feet, her head bobbing up and down as he has *his* cock sucked. The prince holds her head, watching with his mouth parted, then looks up and winks at me, so I roll my eyes at him. As if taking this exchange as a cue, Kay shuffles onto her knees.

So fucking tempting.

I can't see Luc but can hear him behind the chaise that Eli sits on. I smile as I remember the guard's comment—the Emerald Prince and his public fucking. I'm surprised he doesn't have her bent over the back of the chaise so we can all watch.

For the first time, I'm disconnected and disinterested, and I know why. If the others had kissed or touched Ria, would they suffer from the same problem I do? The need for her is eating me from the inside. From the moment her mouth met mine the night I planned to fuck her, she's held my mind and body in a grip I can't escape. Kissing her again tonight didn't relieve the ache at all; the lust for her is more intense than ever.

The First-Borns' connection holds the same unshakable power, these dragons with the purest blood unable to part from each other's mind, body, or soul. The princes are created from that same blood, not through offspring but by the First-Born nurturing their essences into dragon form. The flights' First-Born created us to ensure purer blooded dragon princes hold onto the court and from here we're to breed with those they choose.

By placing their essence in us but constrained by their rules, is this a way to ensure those who're the First-Borns' legacy remain under control?

Until now, the First-Born turned a blind eye to our hedonism, and I honestly believed we'd managed to escape any idea of life bonding. Now the situation with Velanor abruptly ended the possibility we can continue this lifestyle. What if I'm told to bond soon too? Fuck, no.

I never understood the intensity of the bond between Talindra and her consorts, at how a female could hold three men in her grasp—especially primordial dragons. Are they enthralled the way I am with Ria? That the male elders were destined to yield to and meld with their Ruby as I want to with Ebon?

I hold a palm against my forehead. What's Vel doing with Ria? I haven't stopped thinking about the situation since I saw them leave the gathering. I had two choices when I told Ria—allow her to walk into a situation with Vel that could end badly and hope she gets the upper hand, or take her. I tell Ria that I'll protect her and then walk away when she's under threat. How can I do that? I talk of honor, but my desire not to threaten my position in court or risk punishment saw me make the wrong choice.

I should've fucking taken her from that arena.

And then Ria kissed me again and solidified the *other* plans I'm making with or without help from the others.

So, I shouldn't sit here with girls eager to fuck, I should be at the Ruby court in case Vel is serious about assaulting

Ria and her Ebon emerges. If I were Vel, I'd be pissed at how Ria humiliated him in the arena and my temper is nothing like his. I can't predict what he might do.

Before the girl can get her hands on my cock, I stand and cross to the table for more wine.

Somebody pushes through the gauzy curtain, and I turn to tell whoever it is to leave. Vel. He straightens and surveys the room, gaze briefly landing on Eli and the girl with her mouth full then jerks his chin at me in greeting.

He'd dressed differently to earlier—the royal uniform replaced with the loose white shirt and leather pants he favors. Sucking on his teeth, he darts a look from girl to girl as he drinks from a bottle in his hand.

"Thought you were staying in your court, Vel," says Eli. "Surely you didn't bring Ria with you?"

A muscle tics in his jaw. "No. Looks like you've some choice pussy tonight."

"You shouldn't be here," I say.

"Why? I should be with *Ria*," he drawls. What has he done with her? "And don't look at me like that. I didn't fuck her."

Two girls whisper and I shoot them a warning look. "Keep your mouths shut about anything you see or hear."

Vel grunts and wipes his mouth with the back of a hand before resting on the wall. "Who wants to fuck me?"

"No, thanks," quips Eli.

"Vel," I warn. "You're betrothed."

"And?" He smiles at the girl who sits at my feet. "You ever wanted to fuck the Ruby Prince, Kay?"

She giggles, looking at him from under her lashes and I shake my head in despair as she stands. Vel runs his tongue along his lips as she sashays across the room towards him. The moment she reaches him he pushes her against the wall,

225

lifting her skirts and fumbling with his pants as she eagerly wraps her legs around him.

I blink. "Vel. How drunk are you?"

Bracing himself with one hand, I half-cringe as he rams himself hard into her and she buries her face into his shoulder to suppress a scream. Well, Vel is always ready to 'rise to the opportunity'. Fast. Wrinkling my nose, I look back to the ceiling. Vel doesn't fuck in front of others often and is taking a risk doing this on the same evening the First-Born announced his upcoming marriage.

Shoving away the girl trying to replace Kay, I lie sideways on the chaise, feet crossed at the ankles, debating what to do.

I JERK AWAKE AS ELI CLAPS MY CHEEKS WITH BOTH HANDS and I regard him through bleary eyes. "What?"

"Vel's here which means Ria's on her own."

I turn my stiff neck to look around the room. "Where is he?"

"With girl number three. Took her outside."

"Three? Fuck, what's wrong with him?"

Eli shrugs. "At least one isn't Ria."

My parched mouth dries further. "He'd better not be lying about *that*." I swing my legs around.

"Vel isn't an issue now, but I don't know where you can take Ria and not be found."

"Aren't you coming with us?" I ask.

"I don't know." He shakes his head. "I'm not sure this'll work—look what we're risking."

I lower my voice, looking at the girl beside me, passed out drunk. "If we don't all do this, one of us gets fucked over."

"If you want to take Ria, tell the First-Born. You practically won the rite, anyway."

"The First-Born are the problem, Eli." Standing to face him, I slant my head. "Is Luc still meeting us?"

"If he goes ahead, yes." He blows air into his cheeks. "She might not want to go with you, Cam. Or trust you."

"Then let's find out."

"And what if she really *is* our answer to an Ebon threat?" he continues.

"Then treating her like an enemy will have the opposite effect. The First-Born are taking too many risks."

CHAPTER 32

CAMANOR

I MAKE MY WAY BEHIND THE CURTAIN, AND THROUGH THE now empty cantina while Eli looks for Luc. Maybe I'm stupid to do this and will lose everything but I can't watch Ria treated like this any longer. Each time the fear slips out from behind her eyes, something inside me breaks. Then the need to wipe out anything that causes Ria pain escapes, which is a huge fucking problem. If an unspoken bond influences me to this degree already, Ria needs to go before I attack somebody in Reodian. A prince. A First-Born.

"Cam." Vel's gruff voice comes from a darkened corner where he sits at a table, gripping a wine bottle. Drinking and public fucking? Something's bothered him. Before I can speak, he stands and approaches. "Take her."

"Ria?" He nods. "I don't want to upset the First-Born, Vel. They chose you."

"No. *Take* her. Get Aurelia far, far from here. From me."

He sets the bottle down and rakes hair from his face. "She's a fucking sorceress."

He's kissed her. Touched her. Vel can't hide her scent beneath that of other girls—not from me. "What did you do, Vel?" I ask in a warning tone.

"The woman seduced me. Or tried to." I bite my lip. *Ria listened.* "But now she's stuck. Here." He taps the side of his head.

"Did you fuck her or not?" I ask stiffly.

"Not." His jaw tightens. "But the effect... Has this happened to you? Has Aurelia bewitched you?"

"Ah." I half-smile. "That's not sorcery, Vel. That's a bond. A primal one, not one thrust on you by Talindra."

"Bullshit."

"If you've kissed or put your hands on her, she's in you somehow. Same happened to me and every time I touch her this gets worse." I give a wry smile.

Vel's eyes widen in the dark. "No, she fucking isn't. No Ebon witch gets to possess me. We need to get her away from Reodian. From our lands. I never want to see her again, and she can't stay here to weave her magic."

I give a short laugh. Is it safe to tell him my plans? He's definitely changed his opinion that she needs watching. "And what? We tell Talindra she mysteriously escaped?"

"Come on. We can figure something out. Get her out of our lives."

"And our bodies? Minds?" I jab a finger into his chest. "Hate her or not, something in there will always protect her."

"You think?" He sneers. "The others? Have they touched her?"

"Not yet," says Eli as he appears at my shoulder. "What's happening?"

"I want Vel to take me to Ria." I poke my tongue into my cheek. "I want to see that she's safe."

229

"If she were anything but safe, you'd know," retorts Vel. "And no, you can't see her."

My eyes narrow. "Why?"

"She's fine. Sleeping now, probably. Mal is outside her door as usual."

"Then you won't mind if I see her, and I'll ask Mal if he's seen or heard anything... untoward."

He glares at me, eyes glinting in the dim as our gazes lock. Everything between us recently has been conflict. Disharmony in the flights. "Fine. You can see Aurelia if you take her far away."

"Very well. I'll take her tonight,"

Vel snaps his head back. "You would? Where?"

I step forward and cross my arms. "Do you *care* where?"

"No." He glances at the cantina door. "Fine. Find the woman unharmed and get her the fuck out of my sight."

I'M PISSED THAT VEL HAS RIA UNDER GUARD, SHE'S TRAPPED enough without that, but I know Mal is a fair man. He wasn't happy when he thought Ria and I were about to fuck in the dark room, but I don't think he'd let Vel hurt her. Or would he? Even though Vel agreed we could go to Ria, he's cagey. Eli has joined us, but we couldn't find Luc so at least I have one ally who doesn't want Ria hurt.

And is prepared to help me.

We trudge from the Ruby portal room and into the palace, the lanterns dim and nobody around considering it's now the early hours. Despite the long night, I haven't drunk as much as the night by the fire that kicked off all this crap. Eli's burbling about girls but Vel remains tense and quiet.

"You plan to stake the claim you made at the rite?" asks Vel as we wander along the hallway.

I exchange a glance with Eli. "Something like that."

"And if the First-Born lose their shit?"

I don't reply. They won't be able to because we won't be here any longer. I'll take her elsewhere for protection. Head off any conflict between dragons and the other races that this could trigger.

We reach the arched door that leads to the stairs heading up to the guest wing and I watch for Vel's reaction—any worry or guilt. If he's hurt her... Still, he climbs the steps two at a time and ensures he reaches the room first.

"You think Vel did something?" asks Eli softly.

"I'm trusting he didn't, if he brought us here."

Halfway along the unlit hallway, Vel stands facing a door looking between it and the empty bench outside to the left. Believing he's waiting for us before he enters, I stride over.

The door is open, and he stares into a chamber. Ria isn't on the bed. Nor on the seat in the corner. Frowning, I walk to the bathing room. Nobody.

"Where the fuck is she, Vel?" I spin around and I'm in his face in a heartbeat. "What have you done?"

Is the confusion fake? "Nothing. I told you. I want to keep away from her."

He staggers as I slam both palms into his chest. "You've done *something*. Told Mal to take her?"

Blinking, he looks back to the bench outside. "Mal? Where the fuck is he?"

Scoffing, I shove him again. Harder. "Where the fuck is *she*?"

"I don't know!" he shouts. "In the palace somewhere? Maybe she used her Ebon sorcery on Mal?"

"She isn't a sorceress!" I shout back.

"Then where are they?" Eli asks as he grabs my arm before my curled fist meets Vel's face. "Even if Vel isn't involved, they're both missing."

231

I dart over and grab the torn material on the floor by the bed, at first confused. "What's this?"

"Ria's dress."

The heart of what I am bursts free, the dragon taking hold even though the only signs are my claws. Rage overcomes me and I launch myself at Vel, sending him flying into the wall. I don't wait for explanations—there's only one here. Vel did what he threatened.

"I didn't do anything she didn't want!" shouts Vel. "Get your fucking hands off me."

"She ripped her own dress off?" Spittle hits his face as I shout again.

"I told you; the woman seduced me. I joined in. Her dress got ripped." Both of his hands smack me hard in the chest. "When we find her, ask."

"*If* we find her," I snarl.

"Cam!" At the edge of my awareness, Eli's face comes between me and Vel. "We'll look for Ria. If he's lying, deal with Vel then."

"And if we can't find her?" I snap.

"We found her once, we can find her again," says Vel through bared teeth. "And I want to know where the fuck Mal is."

I step away, the fury in my blood cooling. "You genuinely don't know where Ria is, do you?"

"All I know is I left the room, and she was inside. Mal was guarding outside. The door was locked which means he must've unlocked it." He straightens his shirt. "They can't be far."

"You were at the cantina for two hours," says Eli. "That's enough time for one or both of them to go *somewhere*."

"If Ria turned feral and hurt Mal and left, she's no real idea where to go," says Vel.

My heart stutters. "Did you provoke her Ebon? Is that what's happened?"

He scowls. "No. If I had, I would've dragged her in front of you all."

"Then what if Mal took Ria?" I ask. "Because if he's hurt her, you'll both pay."

Vel frowns. "Why would he do that?"

Eli turns from where he stands in the window. "They're both missing and they're either together or one of them is hurt or dead. Whatever the answer, we have a problem."

Tossing Ria's dress to one side, I perch on the end of the bed and stare at Vel. I don't know what happened between them, but he's not telling me the whole truth. There was something off in his behavior earlier. Yet he's as confused and panicked as I am—whether for her or Mal.

I feel sick. I'd decided to help Ria in any way I can, but my fucking stupid decision not to take her with me from the gathering led to a worse situation. There wasn't blood on the floor outside the room but that doesn't mean they're both unharmed.

What the fuck do we do now?

The Dragons Reborn series continues with Wings of Sapphire and Storm which releases in 8th December 2022

Printed in Dunstable, United Kingdom